In this tensely wired, swiftly paced story of human trafficki
nuanced clashing cultures, author Johnnie Bernhard defines each character's motivation
to portray the collision of opposing sides while casting a wide lens on a human atrocity. *Hannah and Ariela* is the story of one woman's bravery in rescuing another, only to rise phoenix-like into a newly defined, far-reaching life purpose.

—CLAIRE FULLERTON, *New York Journal of Books*

Johnnie Bernhard handles sensitive issues of race, migration, and human trafficking with deft and grace as her characters pursue truth and justice. This story is at once suspenseful and profound, raising provocative questions about the lawfulness of laws and the laws of lawfulness.

—ALLEN MENDENHALL, Publisher and Editor in Chief, *Southern Literary Review*

Award-winning novelist Johnnie Bernhard weaves compelling characters into a page-turning thriller. The old adage, "Beware of wolves in sheep's clothing" applies to the cartel character, Ricky, who beguiles Ariela and Katia into making a fatal error in judgment. *Hannah and Ariela* is a brilliant social commentary that needs to be read by every family who loves their children. In Veritas, this fine fictional work does indeed mirror life and serves as a warning to those who may fall victim to predators. In my view, this is Ms. Bernhard's most important work yet.

—MARCI HENNA, author of the Fireside Series, Executive Producer of *When We Last Spoke* movie

Mourning her late husband, Hannah must decide what's next for her and her 640-acre ranch when a shocking discovery on a desolate stretch of road changes everything. Tough and resilient like the west-central Texas land it is born from, *Hannah and Ariela* tells a dark yet hopeful story of two women from opposite sides of the border and the sad and harrowing reality of human trafficking.

— PHILLIPPE DIEDERICH, author of *Diamond Park*

In this literary thriller that involves international borders, murder, and sex trafficking, two women, lost on their own, change each other's destinies late one night. One in her seventies, American, the other a young teen, Mexican. One running for her life and a completely new future, the other a widow, trying to hang on to her old life, full of memories. . . . I loved all the characters, including the play-by-the-rules biracial border patrol officer and the small-town cheese puff-loving sheriff, who form an oddball rescue team.

These trafficking stories play out every single day, with more frequency than ever, along the Mexico/US border. Johnnie Bernhard, a native Texan who now lives in Mississippi, which has the second highest rate of human trafficking in the US, has written a book that will not let us avert our attention. Her words ring off the page with a frank honesty that will move you, and it's my hope they will also move you to action.

—KATHRYN BROWN RAMSPERGER, humanitarian, journalist, and award-winning novelist

The only thing tougher and more beautiful than the Texas-Mexico borderland of Johnnie Bernhard's redemptive novel are the title characters. It would be a better world if we were all as strong as Hannah and as brave as Ariela. This book and these women will stay with me for a long time.

—TIFFANY QUAY TYSON, author of *Three Rivers* and *The Past is Never*, winner of the 2018 Willie Morris Award for Southern Fiction

Like a rose growing out of parched West Texas limestone, Johnnie Bernhard delivers a story of love, hope, and life overcoming hopelessness and darkness. *Hannah and Ariela*, told from the viewpoints of its characters, is a triumph. I'm a fan of Bernhard's books, but this is my new favorite.

—MARSHALL RAMSEY, Editorial Cartoonist and Editor-at-Large for *Mississippi Today*

A narrative tour de force. . . . In this luminously told, multi-voiced story, Johnnie Bernhard depicts an unlikely friendship. Defying expectations, gutsy protagonist Hannah seizes her chance to live beyond the confines of gossip and middle-aged mores. An encounter with teenage migrant Ariela kindles her strength, forging her fierce determination to fight for the fragile and lonely.

—REBECCA COPELAND, author of *The Kimono Tattoo*, winner of the 2022 Independent Press Award in Multicultural Fiction

Audacious! Author Johnnie Bernhard stands front and center, unafraid in her role as truth-teller in *Hannah and Ariela,* her best and bravest novel. . . . In crisp, stark, vivid language, the chapters alternate between key players who speak in first person, inviting the reader deep into the hearts and minds of each person caught up in this tale that deals with human suffering, but also shows humanity at its best. We meet characters as hardy as the hardscrabble land they inhabit along the border between Texas and Mexico, even those unsavory ones who choose cruelty over kindness. The author writes with empathy and compassion, but she does not spare the reader, and in the process, we learn things.

—KATHLEEN M. RODGERS, author of *The Flying Cutterbucks,* NMPW Zia Award First Runner-up

Johnnie Bernard has once again captured the soul of a region, this time through a vibrant array of voices, characters whose integrity and endurance are tested on bristling desert borderlands. Kaleidoscope perspectives carry the reader forward: even the villains and neighbors help weave this story of discovering one's calling and answering it, facing real danger, and receiving real spiritual aid along the way.

—LESLEY CLINTON, award-winning Texas poet

Set in the dual harsh realities of central Texas ranching country and a cartel-controlled rural Mexico, this novel delves deeply into two of the greatest mysteries of the human heart: loss and love. The two main characters, Hannah and Ariela, meet in a dangerous whirlwind of tragedies, sadness, and betrayed trust. Yet through each of their internal strengths and beliefs comes a time of renewal and new love—the greatest miracle of all.

—SARAH CORTEZ, President and Founder, Catholic Literary Arts

HANNAH AND ARIELA

Other books by the author

A Good Girl

How We Came to Be

Sisters of the Undertow

HANNAH AND ARIELA

A NOVEL

JOHNNIE BERNHARD

TCU
Press

FORT WORTH, TEXAS

LIBRARY OF CONGRESS CATALOGING-IN-PUBLICATION DATA

Names: Bernhard, Johnnie, 1962– author.

Title: Hannah and Ariela / Johnnie Bernhard.

Description: Fort Worth, Texas : TCU Press, [2022] | Summary: "HANNAH AND
ARIELA explores life and death along the Texas-Mexico border as two worlds collide
when a seventy-three-year-old widow finds the semi-conscious body of a fourteen-year-
old Mexican national in a ditch along a Central Texas remote byway. The question
of justice for a victim of human trafficking and the woman who helps her lies in the
hands of a biracial border patrol officer and an unconventional small-town sheriff. The
I-10 corridor of Texas connects saints, demons, and victims as the ultimate decision of
life and death are made by two strangers fate has bound together. They must decide to
either follow the law or their conscience to survive"— Provided by publisher.

Identifiers: LCCN 2022004932 | ISBN 9780875658162 (paperback) |
ISBN 9780875658315 (ebook)

Subjects: LCGFT: Thrillers (Fiction)

Classification: LCC PS3602.E75966 H36 2022 | DDC 813/.6—dc23/eng/20220207

LC record available at https://lccn.loc.gov/2022004932

TCU Box 298300
Fort Worth, TX
To order books: 1.800.826.8911

Design by Julie Rushing

To Bryant, my true north.

Cursed be anyone who perverts the justice due to the sojourner, the fatherless, and the widow.

DEUTERONOMY 27:19

CHAPTER ONE

Hannah Schoen Durand

Durand Ranch

Rocksprings, Texas

It began sleeting sometime after 10 p.m. Sleet hit the windows, reverberating within my bones and hips as the rain froze on each pane of glass. That was the first time I woke up. I was still wearing the black dress I'd put on that morning, knowing full well this was something I'd never done in my life, slept in my clothes. I'd just buried my husband. There'd be plenty of new things I'd have to get used to.

I heard Abby stir on the rug near the bed and patted the empty space where August slept until the day he died. "Come on, girl." She put her head on his pillow, releasing a low moan.

The black dress against her border collie fur blurred the division between human and animal. There was some comfort in that. Sleep eventually came and drifted in and out of my body, until I reached across the bed for his hand. It was a cruel realization that I would reach forever without finding him. Fate played a joke on me with forty-eight years of marriage reduced to me alone in a bed with a dog. I would miss the feel of August's hand on my right hip, the low muttering of "good night," vibrating from his chest where my head rested. I would miss him, like a phantom leg of an amputee, aching from a loss never to be filled.

I got up, turned the light on next to the bed, then padded in slippers to the kitchen. Abby followed. While I waited for the teapot to boil, I stared out at the blackness from the kitchen window with the barn and the garage silhouetted from the light of the twenty-five-foot utility pole.

I was thankful August remembered to insulate the well house before the winter storms, but he had always been so good with the seasonal needs of the ranch. The ranch was well managed, although the work got more difficult for us over the years. We sold most of the livestock once he got sick. We kept a few longhorns, Herefords, and sheep. "Just need a little something to look at from the porch," he'd say. It wasn't an indulgence for the man to have that. We didn't play the game of his and hers. I didn't tell him no, and he never once said the word to me.

Sammy was snoring in his childhood bedroom, same twin beds, athletic ribbons and trophies adorning the room. I wasn't much on remodeling and decorating. Always preferred to be outdoors. Leslie insisted on sleeping in the other twin, letting their oldest, Aaron, take the full bed in the room next to mine, while his brother Will slept in August's office on a daybed. She was hard to understand, but I made a point a long time ago not to make my son's marriage part of my business.

Leslie was a good wife in many ways to our son, giving us two healthy grandsons, although we were never close. A San Antonio girl, she never cared for the ranch. She was bored out here, and there wasn't much shopping in Rocksprings. But Sammy came with the boys throughout their childhood, teaching them how to navigate the land and the wildlife. The boys were about grown now; soon they'd be going off to college. The years didn't change the differences between me and Leslie. I respected her, and I believe she respected me. Sometimes that's the most you can ask from an in-law.

A blue norther was howling, vibrating the living room windows. I kept the drapes closed in there, although the day would break in another hour or so. Placing my empty teacup on the coffee table, I reached for August's cracked leather Ropers, still next to his chair, the brown leather recliner I bought him for his birthday last year.

Out in the hall, his coat hung near the front door. I put it on. The sleeves were a good four inches longer than my arms. His smell, a blending of oaks, cedar, and sweat, permeated the coat as I buttoned the large plastic buttons, hard against my thumb and index fingers. I wrapped his wool scarf around my neck and pushed against the wind to open the front door.

When I stepped onto the porch, the wind bit hard, raw, smarting my eyes. I strained to see in the dark. What was I looking for? I kept asking myself. It was ridiculous I was even out here. What if Sammy was up, watching me? He'd think I'd lost my mind. But it didn't stop me. I stared out into the night sky at the stars, remembering when August taught me the names of each constellation, correcting my pronunciation a few times, only to make sure I wouldn't embarrass myself in front of anyone less loving.

They say you're either a preacher or a teacher in this life. He was a teacher, who never wanted me to go through life with only the half-truths of things so infinite and beautiful as a star or the love between a man and a woman.

August Durand. I know you're here. I can feel you in the wind and in the breaking of the cedar branches covered in ice. Hold me just one more time and tell me what you think I should do with the rest of my life, my life without you. Should I sell this place? Don't know if I have it in me to run it alone. For the first time in my life, I feel vulnerable, almost afraid of being out here by myself.

I heard Abby barking, scratching at the door, trying to get out. Just as I turned to go back in, Sammy opened the door.

"Mama, you all right?"

He reached for me, and unlike most of the years of my life, I didn't struggle to be the strong one. I wept shamelessly in my son's arms, finally knowing what it felt like to hit rock bottom.

CHAPTER TWO

Ariela Morales
Zaragoza, Mexico

I didn't hate Zaragoza. My family was here, Mama and Papá, my little brother and the baby. Our little dog Xolotl was part of the family, too. The gringos who came to buy horses from Papá called her Bolt, because she was named after the Aztec god who ruled over lightning and fire. Sometimes I called her that too. It made me feel good to know an English word. Someday I'd know the whole language. I was the only girl I knew in Zaragoza who wanted to speak English, besides my cousin Elena and my best friend, Katia.

My cousin lived just a few streets away. Katia lived by the church. All their houses were easy to walk to if I needed any of them or if I got bored. I always had someone to talk to, someone who knew me and my family. There were no strangers in Zaragoza, except the men and women who worked for the cartel, and I learned as a very young girl to stay away from them.

Like every kid in Zaragoza, I helped my family. I cleaned the house, babysat for my mother, although not for very long, only when she needed to walk to the tienda for a little something or to the church for a prayer intention. No one sat around all day playing video games like kids on *el otro lado*. The other side, across the Rio Grande, was a different world, where kids couldn't wait to grow up, because life would only get better and better.

Life in Zaragoza was hard because it was too close to the Texas border. Those television antennas and satellite dishes on top of our roofs reminded us every day of a better life. Colorful pictures of gringos shopping in malls, talking on their cell phone, living in mansions beamed into our little cinder block houses every day. In *El Norte*, even ten-year-old girls got their nails done. In Zaragoza, you got two opportunities to get your nails done: your quinceañera and your wedding day. Otherwise, you painted your own nails with the polish bought at the tienda near the house, and it was never the same color seen in magazines. Most of the time, half the bottle was dried up, and the little nylon hairs from the brush would fall out when you dipped it into the polish and put it on your nails. You'd have to start all over again with your manicure!

Never, no matter how hard you tried to make the color last on your nails and keep your cuticles pushed back like the pictures in the magazines, it still wasn't half as good as a manicure in a salon. Every time I looked in the tiny salon window and saw pictures of women with long, black hair, wearing evening dresses of white with diamond earrings touching their shoulders and their nails red, I wanted to die! In time, I learned to give up that little dream, just like I learned to give up on a lot of things in Zaragoza. No dinero, no dream.

Little dreams of being somebody other than your father's daughter or your husband's wife just dried up like the nail polish. At thirty, you had your mama's hands and split, dirty nails.

Some people in Zaragoza had a harder life than me and my family. My best friend, Katia, was one of them. Her papá was killed last year, working in the silver mine. The company paid for his funeral and gave a little check to the family, but that was it. No pension for a family of five. Katia, the oldest, started cooking and taking care of her little brothers and sisters, while her mama got work cleaning houses for rich ranching families all over northern Coahuila. Señora Hernández took the little bus in and out of the city every day except on Saturday afternoons and Sundays. Those were Katia's free days. We spent the whole day in town, first going to Mass to get our mamas off our backs, then sitting underneath a shriveled-up oak tree, reading magazines and painting our nails at an old card table someone left behind after a church barbeque. But mostly, we just dreamed about getting out of Zaragoza, sitting underneath that ugly tree.

"You want to do the cavalcade with me and Papá next month? You can wear the white leather chaps, and I'll wear the traditional dress for the parade. Papá can lead us both into town on the quarter horse the Mejía's own. They won't mind. Papá's been working for them so long; they trust him with everything."

Katia didn't answer me. She was concentrating on her pinkie nail, slowing moving the polish brush. She bit her lower lip when the polish brush glazed purple over her cuticles.

"Are you listening, Katia?"

"The cavalcade is a long way off. I don't know what I'll be doing then."

CHAPTER THREE

Hannah
Durand Ranch

"You can't stay here another day, holding my hand. You and Leslie have jobs; the boys have school. It's time to go home. I got a lot of things I need to take care of."

Sammy watched me move back and forth from the stove to the kitchen table where the four of them sat, staring at me, watching every step I took as if I'd collapse any minute.

"You going to keep Joseph on or sell the rest of the livestock?"

"Haven't even thought of that. I was thinking about writing thank-you cards and returning casserole dishes. Now, y'all eat. Eggs are fresh. Sandra brought them over on Thursday." I placed a wicker basket of biscuits on the table in front of Aaron. "Made them just for you and your brother. What you don't eat, take home with you. You can put a sausage patty inside that biscuit and it will do you for lunch later."

"You don't have to wait on us, Hannah. Come sit down," Leslie offered.

"I'm not hungry this morning, but I'll have a cup of coffee."

I sat down at the head of the table, August's chair, with an empty cup in front of me. I didn't know how tired I was until I did, bone-tired and numb. Leslie poured me another cup of coffee, squeezing my shoulder before sitting down.

The boys ate in silence, covering their scrambled eggs with pico de gallo, the jalapeños, tomatoes, cilantro, and onions vibrant in their colors on the mustard-yellow yolks of farm eggs. Sam wasn't eating, only sipping the cold cup of coffee he held in his hands.

"Mama, it just doesn't feel right, leaving you alone on the ranch. It's not

7

just the work that needs to be done, it's the isolation. You're too far from town."

I looked at him without answering. He had his father's high forehead, dark, wavy hair, and strong jawline. Unlike his father, Sammy was developing a middle-age paunch from years of sitting in front of a computer to earn his living.

"Rocksprings isn't the same town I grew up in. Hell, the border patrol has its own office here. Narco is a billion-dollar business. You're too damn close to the border, Mama. You ought to just sell it all and move to San Antonio, near us."

"I'm not selling the ranch, and I'm not selling the few animals I have left so I can move into town."

"I can't quit my job and move here to take care of you," he replied, raising his voice.

"Don't be ridiculous, Sam. I'd never ask that of you. At seventy-three, I think I've figured out how to take care of myself. Now, quit worrying. Y'all need to finish breakfast and get on the road. You don't want to get stuck in I-10 traffic."

I placed my hand over his, resting on the table. "Sam, I'll call Joseph this afternoon, and we'll talk about what needs to be done out here."

"Boys, pick up your plates and put them in the sink. Get your things packed." Leslie stood up from the table, nodding at Sam. "Thank you for breakfast, Hannah."

Still that uncomfortable politeness in her. As if she were speaking to the owner of a bed-and-breakfast and not the woman who gave birth to her husband, the man she'd been sleeping with for over twenty years. But what did that matter at this point in our relationship, or really, to me and the rest of my life. Not much. Leslie would keep being Leslie, and I'd just be her mother-in-law, someone she didn't necessarily love but tolerated for civility's sake.

In another hour, their suitcases were packed and at the front door. I noticed August's rifle was leaning in the corner.

"Did you put that there, Sam?"

"It's on safety. Just leave it there, Mama. You might have a repair man, people out here you don't know. It sends a strong message that you're not vulnerable out here. You know how to use it if you have to."

I nodded my head, knowing it was a good idea, then put my hand on Will's shoulder.

"Bye, Grandma. Please don't be sad and lonely. We'll come back at Easter."

"Goodbye, Will. Do your best in school, honey."

Aaron took off his headphones and hugged me.

"Now, Aaron, don't spend your day playing those video games. Not healthy. You need more time outside." He shrugged at me and put his headphones back on.

I approached her first and hugged her. "Bye, Leslie. Thanks for helping the church women with all the food after the service. Let me make a care package so you won't have to cook when you get home."

"That's okay. We'll pick something up."

I knew she wouldn't eat a leftover if her life depended on it; but again, for civility's sake, I offered the Tupperware and foil-wrapped food to her. Potlucks, buffets, and casseroles weren't eaten by Leslie, although she didn't think twice about letting her children eat something cooked in a micro-wave or delivered at a drive-through window. But I didn't say anything about it, as well as a lot of things involving Leslie.

Sam stood at the door, touching the muzzle of the rifle in the corner, trying to read my mind, afraid to leave me.

"Take care of your family, son. I'll see you soon."

"Mama . . ."

"Don't worry so much. I'll call if I need anything. Need some time to sort through things before making any big decisions. Joseph will help. I'm sure Uncle Buddy will be out here for a meal or two."

I hugged him, but quickly pulled away and opened the front door.

"Bye. Be careful on the road."

He hesitated, then walked away, zipping his parka as the wind pushed him to the Tahoe. I waved and blew kisses to the boys. Will pretended to catch them in his hand, then making a fist of his caught kisses, he placed it over his heart. It was the same sweet game we've played since he was a toddler. Sammy smiled at me, then backed the Tahoe up.

Closing the door, I considered whether I should leave August's rifle in the corner by the door. Then, the silence, a quiet I'd never known in this house, engulfed me.

"Abby."

She came from the living room, where she had been sleeping on the area rug. It gave me a lot of comfort knowing two living, breathing souls were in the house.

"I'll take you out for a bit, then we'll get those breakfast dishes, girl."

We walked out past the barn where the cattle and sheep lay low against the wind. The water trough had a thin layer of ice on it, so I broke it with my walking stick. That stick had been around a long time, saving my life on several occasions, beating a rattlesnake I walked up on or pushing aside prickly pear spines and mesquite thorns. It was a hard country, but it was all I knew.

I noticed four broken bales of hay out by the trough. Sammy must have brought the hay out here for the cattle earlier this morning. I'd need to get Joseph on full time out here, the sooner, the better. He was a good hand, working with August and me out on the ranch for over forty years.

The closer I got to the house, the more I noticed the repairs that needed to be done, especially the front door and roof. That door should have been replaced last year. There was a lot of dry rot there, making it a poor barrier from the outdoors. I could hear the wind whistle through it from the living room. One strong wind and the whole thing would give. Plus we had that hail storm a few years ago that did some real damage to the roof. Later we patched it. I didn't want August disturbed by the noise with a new roof being put on. Two years ago was when he began dying. I saw him slip away a little bit each month. Like everyone and everything out here, there was a season. And it all could change from vibrant to frail in a split second.

Before going back in, I stood on the porch awhile, looking toward the sky, hearing a few crows above me. Abby chased them into the next pasture. I whistled for her, turning my face against the harsh north wind. The sun was going down early; it always did in the dead of winter.

CHAPTER FOUR

Hannah
Durand Ranch

I wasn't always an old woman out here by myself. There'd been a lot of good years here on the ranch, but the best year was when I turned twenty-four, the year I met August Durand.

In my early twenties, I wore my straight blond hair in a single braid that kissed the center of my back. It was a perfect, no-fuss hairstyle for my new life. With a degree in land management, I came home to Junction, taking a job at the Y.O. Ranch, monitoring the watershed and wildlife population. More than forty thousand acres of natural prairie grasses, limestone-bedded creeks, hills, and cedars were my office. Some of my colleagues were turkeys, eagles, blackbuck antelope, axis deer, sika deer, longhorns, and aoudad sheep. I loved every day of my job, despite the crippling heat of summer and the ice of winter. But my life had always been defined by extremes. I was the only woman I knew who worked in land management, but it never crossed my mind not to do what I loved, despite all the gossip about me being a lesbian or running wild with men out on the ranch. I had to live my own life, something my parents taught me a long time ago. I wouldn't change my behavior to suit others' opinions of me.

I lived with my mother and father, never thinking to get my own place after college, because I preferred their company to those of acquaintances and friends. They kept my bedroom the way I left it, although they could have used the extra room for an office instead of the milk crates stacked with folders on the dining room table. Keeping my room was a sign of affection from my parents, who didn't lavish gifts and repetitive praise. Actions spoke louder than words with them. Respect was something you earned. Arlene and Preston Schoen were land people, quiet, and reserved. I loved them and my five older brothers, who lived around Kimble County, trying their best to make a living off of land studded with limestone rocks and an annual spring flood that washed away vegetation, animals, and people. You were lucky if you got a job with the city or county. Government work paid better than digging post-hole fences as a ranch hand or working at the feed store, loading fifty-pound bags of corn for Houston and San Antonio hunters to put into deer feeds. About the most exciting thing that would happen at the feed store was the chance to operate the forklift or look at the new dually trucks the hunters were driving into town for the season.

Steady jobs with paid vacation, retirement, and medical insurance were drummed into our heads during our senior year in high school, not what fraternity or sorority we'd pledge once we got to college. That conversation of privilege was much like the well-intended conversation teachers had with their female students on career goals. I was supposed to be a teacher, maybe even a nurse, but I was my mother's daughter. It didn't matter what those voices said. I became what I wanted to be because of my mother's guidance.

Black mascara and lip balm were my only makeup, as it was with my mother, who preferred working with animals and the land to being a housewife. A lot of people thought her a beautiful woman despite the harsh realities of ranch work, the years of physical labor that showed on her hands and face. Like me, she wore her hair long, but she wore it loose. The thick blond strands faded into grey, but the wildness, thickness of it never changed as she aged. It knotted in the wind or covered her eyes until she tamed it by pulling the mass of hair into a low ponytail, swept to her right shoulder. It was my father's joy, that long, loose hair of my mother. I once saw my father brushing her hair when they left their bedroom door ajar. The intimacy startled the nine-year-old girl I was. I only knew them as mother and father, not man and woman.

Arlene Schoen was the ideal of femininity to me, beautiful and strong. My father's love for her taught me what a marriage should be, sensual and supportive. Their roles as man and wife were not defined by gender roles, but as a partnership forged in mutual respect. Many times I saw my mother pitch bales of hay in the pasture when my father didn't have the strength to do it. Daddy cooked meals, hung clothes out on the line, wiped snotty noses, whatever it took to ease the burdens of his wife and keep their children thriving. They worked side by side, all those years, sometimes digging up limestone rocks when making a fence line or planting Santa Rosa plum trees after Mama believed a little orchard could thrive on the south side of the house. Daddy dug each hole, then Mama filled it with water, dragging the hose along with her, following the new row of trees and my father's shovel. Together, they carefully packed dirt around each tender sapling, then placed rope on opposite sides, tying them to stakes for the support they'd need during that first year of uncertainty. Whatever it took to keep our land and family going, my mother and father did, together.

Their love for each other and our family gave me the confidence to do things a lot of girls from Junction wouldn't do. I'm sure it was the reason I married a man fourteen years older than me. Like my mother and father, I made my own norms. I didn't care what other people thought.

I met August Durand at Crider's, a rodeo and dance hall off Highway 39 on the Fourth of July in 1972. The temperature was in the high nineties that day, but by night, the wind blew in from the hills with no humidity. The rodeo arena lights paled in comparison to the thousands of stars above my head.

Mary Garza, the county barrel racing champion and the valedictorian of Junction High School, rode a white Appaloosa mare in the opening ceremonies with a thirty-by-sixty American flag hoisted to the saddle with her right hand. For that moment, Mary was the most beautiful woman in the world, aglow in white fringed leather chaps with tooled yellow roses in the leather.

"A smart and beautiful girl, that Mary Garza. She'll go far in this world," Mama noted. "Her mother was just as beautiful at that age."

Dad didn't say much as he studied the rodeo program, occasionally saying someone's name out loud he recognized between reading the program and watching the crowd in the stands.

"August Durand's here. Haven't seen him in years. Wondering if he's still out in Rocksprings? Arlene, is that August?"

Mother shielded the last rays of the evening's light with her right hand on her forehead. "Think so. Last I saw him was at the county auction. We bought several Angora sheep from him at a fair price."

Daddy stood up and waved in the man's direction. He was of medium build, I guessed a little over six feet in height, with black hair that curled at the nape of his neck. He waved back at Daddy, then began climbing the bleachers where we were sitting.

"Arlene. Preston. Good to see you." He shook my parents' hands, then looked over at me.

"Don't believe you've ever met our youngest, Hannah," my father said.

"Hannah." He didn't shake my hand but smiled and sat down next to my father.

We watched the rodeo, amused by the rodeo clowns and scared for the bull riders. The four of us became the spectator collective, gasping at each near miss of a bull horn in a young cowboy's leg or stomach. Next was the barrel racing event, always a crowd-pleaser, with local girls pushing their quarter horses at breakneck speed around empty oil barrels. Their hair flying behind them as the girl and the horse became one in competition.

I saw a few friends from high school in the crowd, hoping to meet with them at the dance now that the rodeo was about over.

"Are you and Daddy staying for the dance?"

"We have an early morning. If you want to stay, one of your brothers is walking around here. I saw Buddy and his wife standing in front of the cotton candy stand when we first got here. You can catch a ride home with him, if need be."

"I can give you a ride home, Hannah," August offered.

My dad didn't like this. His eyes narrowed as he looked at August. He never once turned around and looked at me.

"Let's go home, Preston." Mother grabbed his hand, and as soon as the last rodeo contestant was given a ribbon, my father looked at August again and nodded. My parents left me with him, sitting in the bleachers.

"I don't want to interfere if you have plans."

"I haven't any plans."

"I guess your father is upset."

"I'm twenty-four years old, but my father still thinks I'm five. It's a good and bad thing. Most of the time it's good. I'm his only daughter."

We walked the few yards to the dance hall, listening to children playing at the south fork of the Guadalupe River. The last of the day's boaters and swimmers were rushing to shore in the remaining rays of sunlight, the dusk of the Fourth of July.

"What do you do with your time in Junction?"

"I work at the Y.O., full time in land and wildlife management. Just got a degree at the University of Texas. Took a little longer than four years since I worked my way through. I enjoy working outdoors. That's the way I grew up, so it wasn't anything new to me. There's a lot of paperwork, but I love my job. How about you?"

"I've got a working ranch outside of Rocksprings. Mostly sheep and a good-size herd of longhorn. It keeps me busy. Worked in the oil patch. Spent a lot of time on offshore rigs in the North Sea, Gulf of Mexico, later in Africa. The ranch was the pot of gold at the end of the job."

I studied his face as he talked. There was some gray in his hair, but it didn't bother me. I found it attractive along with his strong jawline, high forehead, and brown eyes framed by thick brows. I imagined him to be in his late thirties.

"I can't imagine the working conditions in the North Sea."

"Well, the money was good. Aberdeen was cold, the Gulf hot. I mostly worked, slept, ate, and worked some more. Saved every penny I earned to buy my place in Rocksprings. Would you like to sit down?" He motioned toward a row of wooden picnic tables. "I'll get us a beer."

I sat down and watched the crowd, never thinking to look for an old high school friend or one of my brothers. All I could think about was getting to know August Durand.

He handed me a beer, and we sat at the redwood picnic table talking for hours, about books, wildlife, and ranching. Once the band started playing, it was hard to hear each other. He leaned toward me, the open white collar of his cowboy shirt, the smell of his aftershave, were all I knew despite hundreds of people dancing all around us. The world stopped for me the night I met August Durand.

We never got up to dance but sat together on that picnic table until he looked at the silver and turquoise watch on his wrist.

"Almost midnight. Let's get you home, Hannah. Keep your dad happy."

I felt my skin grow hot from embarrassment, knowing he thought me a child, all the while thinking I was glad we were sitting in the dark where he could barely see me. I stood up from the picnic table, and he reached for my hand as we walked to his truck, together.

He drove me home to Junction, walking me to the front door with the porch light on with insects dancing in circles around its yellow glow.

"If you're free tomorrow evening, I'll come by around seven. Rita Longoria makes the best enchiladas and charro beans at Mi Familia on Main Street."

"Mi Familia is about the best Mexican food around. I'd like that."

He didn't lean toward me for a kiss, giving me only a smile, then walking back to his truck, he turned around and said, "Good night, Hannah." I watched the red glow of the truck's tail lights through the venetian blinds of the living room, all the while wondering how I would ever get to sleep that night.

Our first date at Mi Familia Restaurant got the town talking, and they kept talking until the day I buried him. I suppose I gave them reason to, though after time, I quit listening.

That first date in a restaurant was also the first time a man ever asked if he could order for me.

"Just tell me what you'd like, Hannah, and I'll tell the waitress."

It confused me. Did he not think I was smart enough to order my own meal? Or was it because I was a woman? I was often confused by him in the beginning. I couldn't tell if he was lording over me because he was older and well-traveled.

I dated plenty of men at UT who thought sarcastic remarks were charming. Of course, it was the early seventies, and a college campus was a free-for-all with open sex and lots of drugs. I wasn't used to any of that. Junction was an easy town to grow up in. Life there never prepared me for what I encountered in Austin. Social etiquette and what to expect on a date with a college boy was very different from the boys I dated from Junction High School, who spent hard-earned money on entertaining me, arriving twenty minutes early in the cleanest truck possible. Those boys knocked on our front door and spoke to my mother and father, while those college dates centered on bars and beer on Sixth Street. I had a lot of memories from those days in Austin, and none of them were good, except for the education I received. It was probably the biggest reason I remained single at twenty-four, while most of my high school friends were married with children. Moving to Austin forever separated me from my Junction High classmates. Many thought I felt I was too good to go to a community college or even San Angelo State. I suppose a lot of them thought Austin damaged the small-town girl I was. It made me smarter about men, that's for sure. Growing up the way I did, I didn't know people lied straight-faced to get what they wanted.

My family was quiet. We minded our own business, worked hard, and took care of the land and each other. We learned early on our own actions were what we could trust, not that of a stranger or an acquaintance. I forgot that important lesson the years I was in Austin, and I paid for it dearly, losing trust in men outside of my family. I learned to trust August in time. He was the first man to address me as a lady, not a gal, hon, sister, or daughter, but a lady. The man had good manners, simple as that. He displayed them in a one-horse town restaurant as if he were dining at a five-star hotel in New York City.

When the waitress came to the table, she was dressed in a nurse's uniform dress with matching white shoes and panty hose, a far cry from what people wear in restaurants now, but back then, everybody wore a uniform to do their job. It was a sense of pride, I think, to show up dressed and ready to do your job. Now, I believe people start their workday eating their breakfast at their desk, wearing a uniform of flip flops, pajama pants, and tee shirts. Just crazy when you think how much things have changed over the years. I'm clearly an old woman now, when I reflect on the past being so much better than today. But truly, my past with August was the best days of my life.

On that first date, August looked straight at the waitress, then at me, smiling. "The lady would like the enchilada dinner with charro beans and rice. Guacamole salad on the side. I'll have the tamale dinner. We'd both like a glass of sangria. Thank you, ma'am." He then closed the menu, picked up my menu from the table, and handed both of them to the waitress.

That man made me feel like a woman, but he also respected the waitress by making her job easier and appreciating her service. I've been in many restaurants in my life, all kinds, and seen people treat the service staff ugly, not looking at them, mumbling with their mouth full of chips, barking to the waitress like she wasn't even human. It was worse than bad manners. It was demeaning, showing a lack of respect to act so low. Of course, a lot of people accused August of putting on airs, a rich man showing off. I knew he was sincere. His voice and smile lit up the entire restaurant on that first date.

He always over-tipped waiters and waitresses in small family restaurants. Our first date was when I learned why he did.

I opened my foolish mouth and was immediately embarrassed for myself.

"Twenty dollars is more than ten percent." What a horrible thing to say, I thought right after I said it. Was I trying to convince him I knew restaurant etiquette with that remark?

"She's got bills to pay, same as us."

He stood up, directly behind my chair, and pulled it away, so I could get up. Again, my face was hot from embarrassment, wondering if this first date would also be our last date.

When we got into the truck, I turned to him.

"Please don't think I'm a rude person, August. I guess I'm just trying too hard, too hard to impress you. I'm very embarrassed by what I just said."

"You don't have to convince me you're a good person, Hannah. I knew that when I met you last night. No need to apologize. You'll find soon enough I'm not a perfect man. Made a lot of mistakes when I was young. Reckless behavior, mostly just stupid."

He backed the truck up then headed east on Main Street, toward Schrier Park, at the northwest bank of the South Llano River. He parked underneath the shadows of pecan trees, near a concrete picnic table.

"Hannah, if you don't have anything to rush back home to, I'd like to sit with you for a while."

I smiled and sat on top of the picnic table. He didn't sit next to me, nor did he try to hold my hand or put his arm around me the entire time we sat on top of the picnic table. Instead, we talked about the evening sky and the changing of the weather to early fall.

For a while, it seemed, our conversation was less personal than the night at the rodeo. I was confused, but I waited for him to make the first move. The longer I waited, the more awkward it became until I was sure he was no longer interested in me or this date. He acted almost shy. I was about to burst wondering if he'd ever kiss me, until I simply asked. I was never good at playing games with people. Austin taught me well. I thought dating was a waste of time and degrading, because it certainly wasn't about those sweet exchanges between a boy and a girl in high school. Once you hit twenty, there was quite a different expectation between men and women. I didn't like the guessing game. I just wanted to love one man and have him love me. I wanted what my parents had.

"August, did you bring me out here so we could go parking like two high school kids or did you want to talk about the weather all night? I don't know where we're going with all this."

"I didn't have any preconceived notions. It's a nice spot to sit after a good meal. I'm enjoying your company and the river."

"Am I too young for you, is that it? You didn't kiss me last night, and now we're sitting apart, staring at the river, making small talk. Are we going to be just friends?"

"If we start as friends, good friends, comfortable with each other, we'll make better lovers. I got all the time in the world to wait for that. The last thing I want to be is a fool chasing you."

"I never would think of you as a fool."

"I'm afraid of taking advantage of you, Hannah. Of course, I'm attracted to you, but I don't know your experiences in love, and I don't need to know. For the first time in my life, I've got time to really know a woman. That's something I neglected to do with my first wife."

"You never said you were married. I mean, we talked a lot after the rodeo. You never once mentioned that. That's an important detail to leave out about your life."

"Hannah, your arms are folded across your chest."

"Well, I guess I'm just protecting myself against the next thing you'll tell me."

"I was a kid when I got married. I traveled with my job and left a young wife, really just a girl, alone too often. She found someone to spend her time with. Someone I knew. I nearly killed him. Funny how I never felt like hurting her. It was all about my pride; it was never about the loss of love. I left the town I grew up in because I couldn't take the gossip, or running into them. He married her. They had kids together. To be honest, I don't think about her or any of them anymore."

I took his hand in mine, and we walked down the steep, rocky bank of the river, carefully stepping sideways, step by step, as a trail of gravel fell to the river's edge. I stopped at an area on the river shore, hidden by willows and large boulders, then I let go of his hand, all the while looking at him directly in the twilight, as the last of the summer sky descended into oranges and purples above us. I stepped out of my sandals. He sat on a rock and removed his boots and socks. This time he took my hand, as we walked together into the moving, dark water. Its bottom rocky, sometimes slippery from moss-covered stones.

"Hannah," he said, and I moved toward him. It was there August kissed me for the first time, as the current moved between our arms and legs in the dark water.

Above us, perched on a low-lying pecan tree limb, a mockingbird sang its song. That sound and his first kiss have stayed with me for nearly fifty years.

It wasn't but a few months later, we were married. Just when everyone in Kimble County was convinced it was a shotgun wedding, except for my mother and father, I moved out to his ranch, taking two suitcases, my grandmother's accordion, and my favorite horse, Flame, an intense mare with a fiery disposition and a beautiful autumn coat that flashed red in the sunlight. Flame and my grandmother's accordion were gifts from my family—priceless, as they had both given me such joy over the years. The accordion was all I had left of Grandma, so I made sure I kept her memory alive by playing it almost every night of my marriage to August. She would have loved him.

She taught me to play her accordion the last summer we were together. Our private lessons were over once she was satisfied I could sing and play her favorite song, "Du, Du Liegst Mir im Herzen."

But before I reached that level as a musician, almost every day she corrected my German pronunciation, taking a pencil behind her ear and rapping my fingers on the accordion keys, saying, "It is a love song not a march, Hannah. Do not play the accordion as if it is a separate thing from you. The waltz is a lovers' dance, you must love the lyrics and the accordion as one, playing and speaking each word of the lyric as if there were no greater truth in this world. Now, begin with the second verse, 'Wie ich dich liebe, so, so liebe auch mich.' Imagine speaking those words to the man you love. Even in English, they are beautiful words, 'So, as I love you, so love me too. The most tender desires I alone feel for you.'"

The gift she gave me I gave to my husband, playing her accordion, sitting in a hard-back cane chair on the porch during our first spring as husband and wife. I always asked him if he was bored with the one song, but August returned my question with a smile and a shake of his head. In the summer, I played at night on the porch with a kerosene lamp lit on the table beside me. Late September, as the earth tiptoed into the fall with a full moon riding on the equinox, I played at dusk. August sipped his whiskey in the chair next to me. His boot step counting the three-four time of the waltz. In the winter, the winter of his last breath, I played and sang sitting next to him in bed, where he lay gaunt and motionless, except for his eyes following my fingers on the accordion. His lips mouthing the words, "Wie ich dich liebe, so, so liebe auch mich."

But in the very beginning, that tender first year of our marriage, despite people in town talking about me being a pregnant bride, we taught each other how to love. It was during that time I also learned to ignore the whispers in church and the slander women spoke behind my back about marrying an older man for his money. After all, why did I give up my job at the Y.O., after putting myself through college? Those housewives assumed since I was the only woman working around all those men out there, I must have done something wrong and was forced to leave. Truth be known, I could have worked at the Y.O. forever, but I chose to manage Durand Ranch with my husband.

Within two years, our lives became a structured routine, working together on the land and with the animals, just as my mother and father did. When I stopped worrying about being accepted in Rocksprings after living most of my life in Junction, I gave August a son. The vicious gossip about me as a woman never stopped, but it was the price I paid as the younger, second wife. Although no one around here, much less in Junction, knew the first wife's name or the story of how that marriage ended, it didn't matter. Assumptions were more entertaining than reality. And I started the speculation when I went to Austin and waited longer than the local girls to get married. Then I married a divorced man much older than me. Maybe I was too independent to follow arbitrary rules. Breaking rules was easier than suffering the consequence of not being my own person.

CHAPTER FIVE

Ricky Alvarez

Zaragoza, Mexico

I was conceived in a whorehouse in Acuna, Mexico, across the border from Del Rio, Texas. My papá might have been an enlisted man with the Air Force, a middle-aged deer hunter from West Texas, or a gringo teenager, drunk and frustrated with virginity. My mother worked in Mexico's legalized prostitution zones, *La Zona de Tolerancia*, until she got AIDS, although the *federales* swore there were no problems with STDs in the brothels they monitored through surveillance cameras and regular police patrols. Condoms were provided by the prostitute or the customer, neither a good example for following rules.

I was fourteen years old when we moved back to her hometown, Zaragoza. The federales provided shelters for former prostitutes, so at least we had a place to go. It was in town, not far from the school I walked to. She was dying, and I was growing up, realizing I had two choices in this life with a beginning such as Acuna, Mexico.

I could be a moneymaker, trading on my looks. I knew teenage boys who provided services to men, charging up to $350 American dollars for a few hours of work. The real money was in Mexico City, places like Colonia Juarez and near the Hidalgo metro station, where rich businessmen and tourists gathered to view the male prostitutes. The hours weren't bad, mostly working on weekends, from 10 p.m. Saturday to 5 a.m. Sunday. The only thing wrong with my plan was I needed cash. Cash for a cell phone, cash for travel money. So, I waited. I waited for my mother to die, and I waited for the chance to make money.

Cash money and a cell phone came when I accepted my second choice in life. I became a gang member. My pimp was El Jefe, and I trafficked girls and drugs. I did it for power and money, and one other reason. No one would ever dare to say to me again, "Ricky, *su madre es una puta*, a dirty whore."

I loved my mother and because of that I had a weakness as a gang member. Guilt. A softness in my belly making me cringe each time I stole a girl from her family and took her to El Norte. Sometimes I'd make myself feel better by saying at least the girl would eat every day and have nice clothes to wear. That was more than the Church or Zaragoza offered my mother. No priest or saintly women pulled the drunks off her body and handed her a chicken and a bag of beans to feed her child. When her mouth filled with sores, making it impossible for her to eat, and the fevers never stopped raging, no doctor delivered medicine to treat her. None of them came forward, no teachers, no friends, not even my mother's sister, the official village idiot. Crazy Benita disowned her sister and nephew, the prostitute and her bastard son, when we left the Church. I still saw my cousins, Michael and Veronica. They'd at least acknowledge me, because we shared family traits—shame and poverty. When you grow up hungry and humiliated, you never forget nor forgive.

I stayed in school until she died, only because she begged me to. *"Hijo, sé un buen chico. Ve a la escuela."* She was ignorant enough to think an education would change my life. She dreamed I'd be a college boy, like the ones on television in Los Estados Unidos. She never should have turned it on. It only kept her from facing reality. For me, I learned to hate gringos for having it so easy.

I quit the *prepa* in the ninth grade, a week after I buried her in a grave without a marker. The female pimp she once worked for, a *madrotas*, bought her a casket and gave me a place to live until I got a cell phone and a job with El Jefe. The first real money I made with him I bought my mother a white granite tombstone. Madre Amada was all it said on it. No one needed to know when my mother was born or died, except me.

I was a sixteen-year-old soldier in El Jefe's war against the Mexicans and Anglos. Because I was literate and not a meth head like most of the other soldiers, he gave me a truck to drive, making deliveries on both sides of the Rio Grande. I was also better looking than the others, making it easier for me to pick up girls. I didn't have a mouth of black rot like my new partner,

Aamon. I don't know where the animal came from, but he gave me the creeps.

The other big difference between Aamon and me: I still remembered my mother, how she loved me, telling me I could be anything in this world, if only I'd stay a good boy, working in school until I became a banker, lawyer, or scientist, just like the men wearing suits on television. Then, just like it did over and over again, my belly became soft with guilt, especially when I drove El Jefe's truck with Aamon sitting next to me.

Aamon wasn't born from human flesh and blood. He came from some Aztec nightmare with his skeletal frame and hollowed eyes. His only ambition was killing for our god, El Jefe.

CHAPTER SIX

Leslie Duran

Alamo Heights, San Antonio, TX

I met Sam my senior year at UT-Austin. He was finishing grad school as an MBA. I was clear from the beginning what my expectations were. As an accounting major, I understood money. How to make it, invest it, and spend it. I wanted a nice job, home, and family. But most of all, I wanted to do that in Alamo Heights, about five miles from downtown San Antonio.

I was born and raised in San Antonio, so I held no romantic ideas of life there despite it being a tourist destination for millions. The newspapers were printing stories of dead men floating in the San Antonio River since my grandfather delivered Borden's milk there in the early twentieth century. San Antonio was a rough city: human trafficking, illegals, druggies, the homeless . . . I wasn't raising kids there. People in Alamo Heights didn't have to deal with that garbage. Besides, if I wanted to enjoy the restaurants, shopping, and events of the city, I was five miles away. Sam was okay with that.

With a nice check to begin our lives as husband and wife from August and Hannah, we moved there. Sam worked for a private wealth management company and did well. I worked for a hospital full time near the house until our boys were born. Now, I've got a manageable twenty-hour week, allowing me to be a present parent at their events, something my three-time divorcee mother never seemed to master.

I loved Crazy Connie, her well-deserved name, but our relationship was not typical of a mother-daughter. Under her watch, I was a kid doing adult time, driving when she was too drunk to, forging her signature on hot checks at the grocery store, and meeting lunch-ticket stepdaddies with a smile on my face. Crazy Connie was the life of the party, embracing the ups and downs of life with tranquilizers and cocktails.

After riding a roller coaster with my mother through much of my childhood, I learned early to not take chances. Money was security. And I damn well should vet any husband-to-be with checks and balances on a ledger. Divorces were expensive and messy.

My mother's antics made me crave stability and money. Sam gave me that. In return, I took care of our boys and showed his parents respect. I was a polite woman, despite a lot of people thinking I was cold. When it came to our boys, that's where my emotion was planted. I was a mama bear in my protection of them. I never wanted them to know the childhood I had, so I never talked about it. I visited Crazy Connie on rare occasions, like when she was sober. Taking her to breakfast with the kids was always a safe bet.

As Sam's wife, I was dutiful. He could rely on me. August Durand was also dutiful, taking care of Hannah her entire adult life. She never worked outside of the home, except for a year at the Y.O. Ranch in land management, which still seems like an odd career for a woman, but it was the early seventies, after all, and the Schoen family, as Sam explained to me, were always land people, more than social people.

Now, everyone has a mother-in-law story. Mine is short. Hannah was a martyr. She did everything the hard way, though the Durands were wealthy people. I never saw her spend a dime to upgrade the ranch house or put in a pool for when the boys visited in the summer. She could have done so many things to make life easier for her and August, the family as a whole, but she preferred to work outdoors, hard ranch work, despite the money they had.

I always thought of her as a bit of an eccentric. She had some weird ranch management degree, married a man much older than her, and really just kept to herself. Not much on clothes or running with the girls. Come to think of it, she and August never even went on an Alaskan cruise, like most of their age group. Even Crazy Connie did cruises. Book clubs? Why couldn't the woman join a book club or coffee klatch? Every retiree in Alamo Heights was in a book club and a coffee klatch.

Now, August was dead, and she sat on that ranch all by herself. It didn't make sense. Plus, it wasn't safe being so close to the border. Interstate 10 was nothing but a human trafficking and drug corridor. It had Sam worried, and I hated that for him. There was no reason for any of us to deal with this added stress, but Hannah had to play the martyr. She simply hated "being a bother to anyone."

I'd have to keep encouraging Sam to have her sell the ranch. The boys could use the extra college money. It would make such a difference in their lives if they didn't have to attend a state university like I did. I didn't have a choice. Sam went to UT because he'd never leave Texas. But my boys, they were Ivy League material. Why not give them that chance? Hannah held the keys to their future. I'd just have to convince her and Sam that San Antonio is where she needed to be, in a nice retirement home where she can be with people her own age, enjoying what time she had left.

Why struggle if you have the means? You only get one life, right?

CHAPTER SEVEN

Buddy Schoen

Outside of Junction, Texas

They called me Junior until I was nearly seventy years old. I was named after my daddy, Preston, because it still meant something in those days to name your first born after a family member. Nowadays, people name their flesh and blood after celebrities they never met. But yesterday and today might as well be centuries apart, that's how fast people live now, not thinking or caring, just speeding through life like they have all the time in the world.

August's time finally came just a few days ago. It wasn't easy for me in my late eighties to be a pallbearer, but I was honored to hold the man up on his way to heaven. Hannah, my baby sister, was a good wife to him, all the way until the end, refusing to let a nurse's aide help with the hard work of lifting him in and out of bed, getting him to the toilet, even turning him over in bed when his strength was gone. Hannah was always a hard worker, like our mother, but she was also stubborn—didn't want others doing things for her. Maybe it was just pride she held on to all these years, although I wouldn't say she was a vain woman. She easily could have been with her looks and smarts, but there was no mistaking her stubbornness—almost born with it. She had to do it her way and by herself, even when she was a baby girl.

Out of all the kids in the family, we were the closest. I'd go out to her place and have coffee at least twice a week when August was bedridden. I wanted to come more, but she'd shoo me away like I pestered her. It took me awhile to understand she wanted to be alone with him as much as she could. She was like that even before he was sick. They were a private couple, not because they didn't like people, they just enjoyed the peace they found in each other and the land they lived on. It really was that simple for them. It was something I never knew as a young man, much less as a married man.

Before August got sick, we shared some good meals through the years. Brought all my wives, string of kids along, in all kinds of weather and degrees of uncertainty in my own life, but Hannah and August always accepted me, no matter the circumstance. That's the kind of people they were. They minded their own damn business and thought enough of others to let them take care of their own affairs without butting in. If they offered you help, they didn't want to know why you were asking or why you couldn't do a better job taking care of yourself. I never saw either one of them wear their faith like a badge or a means to lord over others. Hannah and August were just good people in about everything they said and did.

I got along with August, although my father never warmed up to him. My brothers didn't care too much for him either, said he robbed the cradle like a spoiled, rich man. The men in the family thought Hannah was pregnant and had to get married, since it was just a few short months between August coming out to the house for her, then the next thing we know, Hannah's sporting an engagement ring. I knew better than that. Hannah wouldn't marry any man unless she loved him, baby or no baby. She also knew she could support a child without a man. And the family would be right there beside her and that baby. Hannah was her own woman, always had been, following the convictions of her heart, not what people thought.

Mama never once mentioned the possibility of Hannah being pregnant to me and my brothers. She never gossiped among us, never picked favorites or asked us to choose sides. That was a nasty business among some families I knew. No one ever won at that. Mama gave Daddy a few harsh looks when he grumbled about August being so much older than Hannah. I imagined she set him straight behind closed doors. The only thing I remember her saying during the time was Hannah was a grown woman with a good mind. Mama never mentioned August's age, either. She treated him like one of her own children from the day he married her daughter. Daddy didn't do that. I don't think he ever got over losing his baby girl. Once my first girl got married, I understood. It was the day I realized the future was moving forward, leaving me behind. That preacher was dead straight when he asked who was giving the bride away, so I put my daughter's hand into the hand of another man and sat down.

Hannah knew what she was doing, marrying August. He loved her and she loved him. We were raised to have confidence in our own decisions, though I often paid for the poor ones I made.

I understood Hannah better than my brothers—hell, better than most people who grew up with her. I never accepted she was just a girl or the baby of the family. I was ten years old when they brought her home from the hospital, and I already knew she was the best of my mother and father.

In a few years, I'd come to understand her intensity—nothing and no one would stop her from doing what she wanted to do. She was just like Grandma Schoen. Of course, Hannah was her favorite. Hell, Hannah was everybody's favorite, being the only girl and all. But she and Grandma had a special relationship. They shared that same iron will in getting stuff done.

Grandma Schoen was brought up on a small farm house outside of Junction. Old folks called the area the Divide then. It was the middle of Texas between those high lonesome plains in the Panhandle, all the way to the coastal flatlands of South Texas. The Divide had the rolling hills, what everybody calls central Texas or the Hill Country. Funny how I remember all this because I wasn't much of a student, but a high school science teacher explained it as natural erosion during prehistoric times, oceans washed across the land mass later known as Texas. Those oceans cut canyons into pieces of limestone. Those same limestones were scattered throughout the area, more common than a blade of grass. Made it damn hard to put in a fence post or a home garden. So, you got to be a tough hombre to live out here with no rain and rocky soil.

Well, my Grandma Schoen was tougher than any hombre or woman I ever knew. You wouldn't know it by looking at her. She was an old woman even when I was a kid. In my mind's eye, I remember her wearing lace-up boots and a cotton house dress with an apron tied around her waist. The only time she wore something else is when she went to church.

She was steady as the day is long, and strong for a woman raised on little food and hard, physical labor. When she was no more than seven, she rode her horse to the schoolhouse in town, almost nine miles away. She carried her lunch of a biscuit with syrup in a little tin pail. If times were good for the family, she had a piece of sausage for her biscuit. It would have been the same lunch for her younger brother, Rudy. And probably the same lunch as her father, and great-grandfather, Arnold Schoen, who was hanged from a tree when he refused to join the Confederates early in the Civil War. They were not people who followed the crowd, much less the squawk of a politician. They learned early on in the Divide to trust their gut.

Hannah's determination was inherited from Grandma, really all the Schoens. I loved her for it, just like I did my grandma. I could count on those two women to always be there when I needed them.

I got along with August, too. We were about the same age, but that's where the similarities ended, except for our love of the land we were raised on. I guess the biggest divide between us was money. He had it, and I didn't, but he never made me feel less a man for it. He was just that type who treated the janitor and the banker the same way. Money just slipped out of my hands, like wives, I guess. Back when I was young and wild, I spent it as fast as I could, because I loved women and riding bulls. It wasn't a vocation you'd get rich on, much less keep a wife happy.

My grandson in Houston called me a rock star when he figured out the scar running from my forehead to my right check was the hoof print of a bull. Took me awhile to laugh about all that, but now I tell all my grands, that's how I got sense knocked into me. It always makes the little girls scream! They didn't need to know their granddad was a crazy, hell-bent bull rider up until the age of twenty-seven, when the 2,200-pound bastard threw me, piercing me in the gut with a horn and nearly caving my face in with his hoof.

I see my family quite a bit now that Alice is gone. Alice was my third wife and best one; of course, I had to suffer with two of 'em before I knew what a good woman was. It would have saved me a lot of money and heartache if I'd been smarter when I was younger. But when you're eighteen and in lust, it can easily be confused for love. That's what I did, married women I lusted for! And that little bit of happiness was long gone by the first year of marriage.

By the time Alice came along, I had all the smarts of a man used and abused by his own mistakes. Alice and I were married for the longest, and she took in my other two kids when my second wife left me with 'em. I never minded being a daddy to my kids. It was the reason I got up and went to work, no matter the broken bones, ribs, or heart. I was used to moving forward each day with an empty billfold. My kids kept me going my whole life, the reason I'm still here. Alice treated them just like the three we had together. No difference. Ever.

She had a bad stroke about five years ago and never recovered. We tried the little exercises the physical therapist taught us, but her right side stayed limp. It was her dominate side, meaning she couldn't sew, tend to her garden, visit her kids and grands, nothing except lie in bed and wait to die. I cried like a baby when she did.

The nights are still bad without her; I guess the mornings are too, but I keep moving. Got a little companion with Rusty Bucket, a one-eyed yellow cat I got from one of my grands. We keep busy with little chores around the house. Rusty even goes to town with me, riding on the bench seat. He never leaves the truck, whether I go into the grocery store or get a bite to eat with one of my kids.

It is still hard to fill all those hours without Alice. The quiet can about kill you. Hannah's going to learn about that, too. And it won't be easy for her. She built her whole life around August, and truth be known, she loved him more than anything in this world.

They kept that spark of interest men and women have when they're young and attractive, all the way up until he died. She loved him like he was still thirty-something and he loved her like she was still that twenty-four-year-old girl with light in her eyes. That face didn't have an etching of grief or worry for many years because of how that man took care of her, loving her more than anyone else in this old world.

She'll have to rely on her stubbornness, now. Just that steel will of hers to keep moving, getting up in the morning, riding out those hours, until sleep comes from boredom, and if she is really lucky, exhaustion. My sister will need to be braver than she's ever been in her life.

It's been on my mind since getting up this morning to give her a call. I have an idea how we can keep an eye on each other, without scaring our children to death. Out here on the ranch Alice and I made, well, not much of one, with only a hundred and twenty-five acres. I'm about thirty minutes from family in Junction, but I'm a good hour drive to Hannah's place. There'd be no way I could get to her in time, if she had any trouble. I'm an old man, and my night-driving days have been gone a long time. My kids and grands do most of my shopping, bringing what I need out to me. But Hannah doesn't have anyone, much less someone stopping by once a day to see if she's okay. I don't think that ranch hand of hers still works out there every day.

But what I can do for her, as well as her helping me out, is agree to a time each morning we can call and make sure the other is still kicking and breathing into the new day.

The god-awful truth is I can't tolerate the thought of her lying dead on the floor or in bed for days 'til somebody comes out and finds her. She has no daily visitors. Sam came for a few days after the funeral, but he won't be around much now. The first time I met that daughter-in-law of hers, I knew Hannah would see her family only on holidays if she was lucky. She is alone in this world with August gone. Calling her every morning after that first cup of coffee would be an easy thing to do. It would make me feel a whole lot better about the situation she's in.

I sat down at the kitchen table, where my cell phone was. Crazy thing. Some days it worked, some days it didn't. I'll be damned if I spend another dollar on it. Used to be able to make a house note for what I give AT&T each month. Hannah picked up on the third ring, just like she always did.

"Buddy, how you doing this morning?"

"Morning. I've been thinking about you being out there alone, and I have a proposal that could help us both out."

She laughed softly, waiting for me to make my big speech.

"Hannah, I know you're an early riser, just like me. Why don't we give each other a quick call by eight a.m. every morning, just so you know your brother here made it through the night."

"Now, Buddy you probably got every widow woman in the county bringing you breakfast by eight every morning, so there's no need for me to check up on you."

I didn't want to tell her, but I had to, and it was best she heard it from me than from some well-meaning biddy out there.

"Hon, there ain't nobody coming every day to check on you. You don't have any family here, except your brothers, and you know I'm the only one you can depend on, but I'm an old man. Some days I can't get out there, but I can call you, Hannah. And if you don't answer, I'm coming, or I'll send one of my kids out. Ain't no big deal for me, like it would be for Sam."

There was silence on the other end. I'm sure it hurt her, but it was something I couldn't beat around the bush about.

"Hannah, you there?"

"I'll call you every morning at eight a.m., Buddy. Thank you for being thoughtful. I guess this is my new life, whether I like it or not. Please don't worry. I'll get the swing of things in a month or two. It's just that I had him for so long, my whole life, really."

"Yes, you did, Hannah. He adored you, too. It'll be okay in time. You're a strong woman, but you should take some time for yourself and rest. Don't overdo. We'll talk in the morning."

"Night, Buddy."

She hung up first. I knew she probably was walking around in circles in that house, burying herself alive with the memories. Sometimes you can love a person too much, building your whole life around 'em, 'cause there's nothing better than time spent with that person. It's an easy safety net we're lured into, thinking that life and that love will be around forever. Well, Hannah did that for August. She never saw him slow down and age like the rest of us. Might have been a bit of denial, 'cause she couldn't accept him leaving this world without her. When he did go, he took half of her with him. And what was left of her was very alone in the middle of nowhere, Texas.

CHAPTER EIGHT

Joseph Gonzales
Durand Ranch

I was sixteen years old when I came to work for August and Hannah. Mostly cleared cedars during spring and Christmas break if there wasn't a burn ban. Otherwise I'd mend fences and do other odd jobs on the ranch. I was a junior in high school and drove my old man's stick shift Ford out to their place. It was just a few months after he died. A calf tied to a supporting beam in the barn yanked hard enough, and the hundred-year-old roof collapsed on the calf and my father. Broke his neck and his back in two places. He died a few days later. The calf survived with two broken legs until I put him out of his misery with a shotgun shell.

Once Dad was gone, we were like every other poor Mexican in town, renting from the Wyatt family who owned a row of shacks off Main Street, where grassy lawns and trimmed hedges were a pipe dream in some Disney movie.

Mama didn't always have the rent money for Dean Wyatt when he'd come driving up the middle of the yard, collecting rent checks without having to get out of his truck, with his teenage daughter sitting next to him. I went to school with his daughter, Pam. Blond, white, American Barbie. I guess old man Wyatt was teaching her the ropes early, as the rightful heiress in squeezing money and managing the peons.

When Mama was more than a week late on the rent, he'd come by himself. Cussing her as if it were her fault motel maids were underpaid. I hated the man since I could remember, wanted to kill him since I was twelve. That's how old I was when he shot our dog dead in the front yard. He was pissed our rent was two weeks late. I cried and cursed him until my mama pulled me inside the house.

35

"Hijo, I'll get you another dog. We'll go now, but you cannot talk to that man like that. He'll kill you, shoot you dead in the dirt just like the dog. We are nothing to him, nothing but sixty-five dollars in rent money. Hardly worth the trouble of speaking to. Don't ever forget that, Hijo."

The Durands were different; my family knew them for generations. My great-grandfather worked on the original Durand Ranch in Castroville in the nineteenth century, although our people were here long before Henri Castro brought the French immigrants to the Republic of Texas and set up the Alsatian culture here, like it was the only one that mattered.

My people were farmers and ranchers on the Medina River, trading goods and animals in San Antonio, a hundred years before the white European showed up, claiming to discover our land. We were here before the Republic of Texas became an Anglo dream.

Little Alsace is what they call it now. *Cabrónes*, all of them, thinking the world didn't exist until they showed up. But the Durands weren't like most of 'em. August always paid me on time, a good wage. Decent people, especially Hannah.

"Save my oaks, Joseph. The cedars are choking them out," she'd say to me when I worked out there, bringing me coffee in a thermos if it was cold out or iced tea in a large Ball canning jar if the temperature was above the seventies. Sometimes she'd join me with a pair of wooden-handled loppers in her hands, dressed in one of August's old shirts, her jeans tucked into cowboy boots. That blond hair of hers always in a braid down the center of her back.

She was a good-lookin' woman back then. Still was. I married a woman the opposite of her. Elizabeth was sixteen years old when I took her virginity. I wasn't but a few months older. She was just a girl I'd known since I was a boy. I suppose it was expected of me to do that, just like it was for me to never date anybody else and to marry her when she told me she was late. The baby was mine, and I took the responsibility like a man. I've done the work and worry of a man since my father died. Feeding a wife and baby didn't scare me, but most of what I did for Elizabeth was out of obligation, not love. She never acted surprised or hurt, just accepted what I offered her in those early years. Elizabeth loved me then.

I didn't love her, although we've shared the same bed for over forty years and raised three daughters together. I loved being a family man, though, working hard for my girls. It gave me a lot of pride to take care of them, something my mother struggled to do for me and my brothers. I wanted them to have everything I didn't. Give them the chance to make a living with their minds, instead of their muscles, like me. I never regretted the work; as long as they had a better chance in the world, it was all worth it. Then the girls did something all children eventually do to their parents, they moved out and started their own lives. When that happened, I realized my marriage to Elizabeth was nothing without the family. Two people and a dog living together made a cold house for me. I tried to stay away from it as much as I could.

I see my daughters raising their young families with my sons-in-law working beside them, but things are different with this younger generation. They're busy, all the time, too busy for me, or especially, Elizabeth. Everybody worked now. Everybody had a schedule, even the children. I got it, but it only made Elizabeth sadder, sometimes angry, gossiping about one son-in-law over another, keeping her girls from her, ruining the family she sacrificed her life to build.

She spent most of her day and night watching television, waiting for her cell phone to ring, inviting her over for a scheduled visit with one of her daughters or a grandchild. I knew my wife felt lost, but I didn't have the energy or desire to find something to keep her going.

Hannah had a sense of purpose, though. What that was, I couldn't put into words. But I could see it in her, how she carried herself out on the land and in town. She didn't withdraw from life into a cell phone and television. She spoke to men the same way she spoke to women. No games with her. I always thought that kind of confidence in a woman was sexy.

When I was a kid, I'd see her and her family sitting together at the Vigil Mass. Young woman, little boy, and an old man. August didn't say much. He was quiet in his ways, and so was she.

A lot of women gossiped about her then. Called her puta, gold digger, the reason August's first marriage ended in divorce. Hannah never acted like it bothered her, but then again, she was quiet, the rare woman who minded her own business.

Hannah and August didn't flinch when everybody got up for communion during Mass except them. The church never recognized their marriage, but by the time their boy was born, we had a new priest, Father Dworzak. Father baptized Samuel, and no one said a thing about it except how much it probably cost August.

Quiet. That's how they lived. In time, most people grew to respect them, mostly because Hannah and August were the reason a lot of people ate during bad times. Women still didn't like her much, except for my mother.

I wouldn't call them friends, but there was a silent agreement between them for years. Mama made their Christmas tamales each year, and each year August ordered more than they could eat, always paying in cash. He'd take a white envelope from his coat pocket with her name printed on the outside, Señora Gonzales, and place it on the kitchen table. Next to it, Hannah left her a Christmas cactus, sometimes a poinsettia.

Just like August and Mama, you think people like them will never die, they're so much a part of everyday life, like the oaks on the land, deep rooted and unbendable. But death came for them like it did for everybody. Mama and August were buried within six months of each other.

Hannah called me a few days after his funeral. Come out to the ranch for some lunch and business, she said. I didn't know what to think of that. I didn't do that much work for them anymore, once they sold most of the livestock. I thought she might want to live near Sam now. She might want to sell the ranch and what was left in machinery, tools, and cattle. I didn't really know what she wanted. She was one of the few women I'd met in my life I couldn't read. Those green eyes were focused on something other than hiding a lie.

I knocked on her front door, same as I had for nearly forty years. She opened it with Abby next to her.

"Joseph. Come in. I'll get us some coffee."

She started for the kitchen, leaving me to close the door. That's when I saw it, August's 30-06. I remember the day he bought it. It was an expensive gun. Later, once his eyesight began to fail, he put a high-powered scope on it. Why she had it out here, right by the front door, I couldn't figure out.

I didn't say anything to her that day, only because I could tell she had lost some of her confidence. Her hair was loose, that thick, single braid gone somewhere in the greyness of her uncombed hair. She walked slower, unsure of her steps. An unsteady hand poured coffee into the mug. Maybe the rifle gave her a sense of security. It wasn't my place to question her. But thinking back now, I should have.

"Wonder if you'd be interested in taking on more work, Joseph? I'd like a spring garden, think it would be good for me, but I'll need you to build a fence high enough to keep the deer out. I want a little wooden bench near the gate, so when my brother comes out here to poke around, he'll have a place to rest in between picking my vegetables! You know Buddy. Never had a shy bone in his body."

"Yes, ma'am, I can take care of it, even the bench for Buddy. Probably start with the bed in February. There's a lot of rock in the soil. Will take some time working it, adding compost. Do you have a place in mind?"

"August loved that spot past the pecan trees. Surprised we never dug another well, thinking how much water he kept on them to keep them alive. You know he loved the papershell the best. Cracking them with that old handheld thing on the front porch in late October, November. Never would let me buy him a decent sheller."

She kept staring out at the kitchen widow, like she was expecting him to walk past, carrying a plastic bucket full of pecans he just picked up.

"When I'm done with the soil, I'll put a fence up, one with a gate."

"Thinking I'll mix vegetables with some flowers. Marigolds help keep the bugs out. That's how my first garden was out here. You probably don't remember."

"No, ma'am, but you can plant what you want as soon as the soil's prepped."

She was still staring out the window, only responding to what I said with a nod.

"Hannah, is there anything else I can do for you while I'm here?"

She turned toward me, those eyes, that terrible sadness within them. It was then I realized I had been in love with her since I was sixteen years old. Elizabeth was right. There wasn't a time in our marriage she hadn't accused me of this. I just pushed those feelings back inside me for so many years I thought they were hidden.

Once my daughters left, there was nothing to stop me from thinking about Hannah and how I used to feel when I was a younger man. That's the cruelty of age. The heart never forgets the longing, no matter how many years go by. I just turned sixty. Hannah was seventy-three. Those were facts I had to accept. The best I could do for her was take care of the ranch and never burden her with my desires.

CHAPTER NINE

Ariela

Zaragoza, Mexico

I hated when my best friend Katia ignored me with little remarks about having such a busy social calendar she couldn't make time for the cavalcade or even give me a hint of a maybe. These things had to be planned, and I didn't like to make more work for Papá by telling him maybe we'd go, and maybe we need two horses from the Mejia's ranch. I would ride Rosa, my favorite mare, and Katia could ride that stubborn Octava who ran like the wind when she heard music. They suited each other, stubborn and wild. I wish Katia would make her mind up, though. She was always trouble, never making a plan, living every minute based on what she liked or disliked that particular moment.

She kept painting her nails, hogging the whole bottle, even though I paid for it. But I couldn't stay mad at her. She was my best friend, even though she drove me crazy.

Father Sánchez came out on the porch of the church, looking across the grassless lot at us. He was probably shocked we were painting our nails in front of the church, since he was always lecturing Katia on being modest . . . chaste, more like Our Lady. I could see his frown from where I sat at the card table. Father was tolerant of me, but he didn't even try to hide how much he disliked Katia.

Staring with disproval at her tight tee shirt across her fourteen-year-old body, and the way her blue jeans fit across her hips and butt, Father never missed the chance to tell her how much he disapproved of her. My mama didn't like her either, saying she was wild, even before her daddy died. But I knew Katia better than all of them. I knew she covered up her fear, fear of hunger, fear of poverty, with the boast of her body. It was all she had

that belonged to her. She had pride in her appearance, even though Father
Sánchez said pride was a sin. "Look to the Virgin Mary for guidance in
humility, Katia." He never said a word to me, but I didn't give him the
chance, either. I'd rather poke my eyes out than look that priest straight in
the face. Katia just laughed at him. "God bless you, Father," she'd say with
her full lips covered in shiny pink lipstick. Sometimes she'd even wink at
him. I got scared when she did that, thinking we'd better get out of church
before it fell on us.

The Vigil Mass was no different than any other Mass, as Father and
Katia continued their little battle from the moment we walked in, until
we were the first to leave. What made it unusual was the new Ford truck
parked by the little tree near the church entrance. It was a double cab truck
with big tires and a glittery red paint job. No one in Zaragoza drove a
truck like that, not even the ranch owners. It was a truck driven by a cartel
member.

I knew one of the boys standing outside of it. Ricky went to *preparatoria*
with me and Katia, until he dropped out in the middle of the ninth-grade
year. He didn't have an easy life, even in those days. The gossip on the
streets was his mama was a prostitute. When she died, he went to work for
the cartel, driving drugs and people all over the place. The stories were wild
about Ricky. He was bad.

I was forbidden by my father to talk to him or anyone else who worked
with the cartel. It wasn't like I'd be punished by having something taken
away for a day or two; my parents would beat me in their frustration to
save me from a world without a right or wrong, where power and money
were made with a machete and a machine gun. My mother knew all
about Ricky. Any time she saw him or his truck in town, she'd make
the sign of the cross and say under her breath, "That boy made the devil
his best friend for a cell phone and a truck. *Legiones de demonios, triste,
triste.*"

Katia didn't care if anyone saw her talking to Ricky, just like she didn't
care what Father Sánchez thought. What difference would it make for her
to keep her family proud or her name honorable? A good reputation for a
fatherless girl and an absent mother without any money might get her into
a convent, married to Jesus, but Katia lost favor with the Church the day

her hips and breasts developed a curve, things she didn't hide or feel shame for.

I stood as far away from the truck as I could without looking like I was abandoning Katia. She was practically sitting behind the steering wheel; she was standing so close to it with Ricky and the weird boy standing next to him. They kept looking her up and down. Of course she knew they were undressing her with their eyes, but she didn't care. She was too busy looking at that truck, pushing her hair from her face, then braiding it, tying it off with a rubber band she always wore around her wrist.

"Get in. I'll even let you drive a little bit, Katia. We're friends, no need to think about what people will say. The widows are tinted. Old witches in this town won't see you," said Ricky, reaching for the door handle. "Ariela, quit acting like a scared chicken. You've known me since we were kids. We'll get something to eat, maybe take you girls to get your nails done in the shop near the taquería. Get what you want. Those little rhinestones on the pinky finger, one on every fingernail if you want. I made a lot of money yesterday. Right, Aamon?"

I was staring at Katia's face the whole time, trying to know what she was thinking. Then I looked at the boots Ricky and his skinny friend were wearing, expensive exotic boots, like the hunters from Texas wore. Papá said they'd show up at the ranch and hunting lodges outside of town, wearing alligator, lizard, even ostrich skins wrapped around their feet. He said those boots were the most expensive he'd ever seen men wear. I kept thinking what kind of evil did Ricky and Aamon have to do, so they, too, could wear expensive boots. How many people did Ricky hurt so he could drive a fancy truck around in the dirt, just to show off to poor Mexican girls like Katia and me?

Those things they dangle around like magic to poor girls' eyes cost a lot of money, more money than all the old furniture and clothes in our house put together. Even if I put Papá's old truck parked in the shed along with those things, it all still was worth less than what Ricky and his creepy friend wore on their feet. The truck Ricky drove could have bought six houses for families in Zaragoza.

"Come on, Ariela. Get in the truck. We'll be back in a little while, way before your Papá comes looking for us." Katia jumped in the truck, taking the driver's seat, with both hands on the steering wheel.

"Sit by your friend, *cariño*, in the back. I can't let you drive until we get out of town, Katia. Don't want you running into a tree or house," Ricky joked.

Katia climbed to the back seat and opened the door for me. It was then I looked at Aamon. His hair was dirty, matted like a little rat's nest in the back of his head. I couldn't see his eyebrows, because his black bangs covered his forehead and most of his eyes. He met my return with an opened mouth laugh, revealing sharp-edged, black teeth, like rows of little daggers and coffins. Even I knew what caused that. Speed. Glass. Meth. But I got into the backseat of the truck anyway, closing the door behind me. When I looked out the back window, Father Sánchez was standing underneath the broken cross in front of the church, staring back at me.

CHAPTER TEN

Hannah

Durand Ranch

I dreamed of our honeymoon, all those years ago in Paris. The slant of light from the closed venetian blinds seeped through the dream, awakening me with the longing I felt in this empty bed for the time I shared with August in the City of Lights.

We were young, walking hand in hand along the western end of the tree-lined Champs-Élysées. The horse chestnut leaves, golden and red, danced before us as we kicked them with our boots, laughing and talking, stopping to kiss, laughing and talking of nothing and everything as we walked hand in hand, Mr. and Mrs. August Durand. On that cool autumn morning, his words were suspended in the damp air, lingering long enough for me to touch them with my fingers, even brush against them with my lips as they floated around me. An October honeymoon in Paris he gave me, whispering in my ear the first night we were there, "The tourists have all gone home, Hannah. We'll enjoy the city like Parisians."

I stood up, pulled the covers across the empty marital bed we once shared, remembering a picture from our honeymoon morning in 1973. I kept it wrapped in a lace handkerchief, stored in an old jewelry box in the closet. I had to see it, before I did anything else this morning. I carried the vanity stool from the bathroom, stepped up on it, reaching for the shelf above August's shirts, and felt the embroidered top of the octagon-shaped jewelry box, a birthday gift from my father when I turned sixteen. Inside were my high school graduation ring, a pair of turquoise earrings, and the wrapped photo.

It revealed a couple very much in love, standing in front of the Arc de Triomphe de l'Étoile. My hair was loose on my shoulders with August's right arm draped around it, smiling into the camera's lens. I remember the French woman who took the photo. She was standing just inside the Arc, waiting for the morning rain to subside, smoking a cigarette. I was embarrassed when August asked her to take the photo, but her smile was quick with the spoken words, "Bien sûr."

I took Spanish in high school and college, although most of the girls I knew were uttering, "Parlez-vous français?" with a distinct Texas drawl. Spanish served me well on my job at the Y.O. Ranch. I immediately gained respect from the ranch hands when I addressed them in their native language. The sorority girls I knew in college took their French speaking skills along with a Julia Child's cookbook and whipped up a soufflé and husband. Language skills required for two different jobs, I suppose. Funny how life works.

I never thought I'd go to Paris. But despite all the things I heard in Junction about the French being rude and eating only frog legs and snails, the people I met there were kind. I felt like a small-town country girl from the wild, wild west of Texas in the sophistication of Paris.

I wrapped the photograph in the handkerchief and returned it to the jewelry box. For the duration of a dream, I had him beside me. From the memory of an old photograph, I felt his touch, but as the morning light grew brighter, I realized the need to fill the rest of the hours in this day with the insignificance of being a widow. When I went to the bathroom to wash the sleep from my eyes that is what a saw, a widow woman with gray hair and arthritic hands. It was only when he was alive did I see myself through his eyes, a pretty, young wife.

Then the filling of all the hours began with the security of routine. I turned on the coffee pot and gave Buddy a call for our agreed eight a.m. safety check. Afterwards, I stood at the kitchen window staring out at the cold January day, then decided a brisk walk with Abby would be good for both of us.

We walked to the back pasture, near the barn, where a grove of trees stood. There were a few bright red leaves left on the Spanish oaks, although their bark was bruised by the rutting of bucks and their limbs bent by the storms of summer and the ice of winter. Yet, that deep red color served as a sign of life among the short, leafless scrub oak and the silent evergreen cedars.

Abby finished her business and I walked back toward the house with her, all the while thinking, *Now what do I do?* Silence was the predictable reply, as I looked at the sun still low in the morning sky, accepting the fact only two hours had passed since getting out of bed. There's a certain loneliness, knowing no one needed me, when my entire life was spent nurturing and loving. I had time, yes, lots of it, but time without someone you love is a burden. I whistled for Abby, and she followed me back to the house, just as unsure as I was about the rest of the day and all those hours to fill.

The only comforting part of grief was being lost in memories. The present was too painful to bear alone, but the past was rich with whatever I chose to remember. So I spent the day remembering him and Paris. It was the only time in our married life we lived completely for each other. We were selfish with every hour, knowing we'd never be that far away from the responsibilities and give-and-take of ordinary life, that exhausting two-step dance of living simultaneously in the past and present, while time disappeared right before your eyes. It was as if we understood we would never live as intimately in the present again. Just once in those beautiful two weeks together I opened the door to a time August was with another woman, even after swearing at the river on our first date we'd never talk about his first wife again, but jealousy is a bitter fruit, with a lingering aftertaste.

I wanted him to say I was prettier. Smarter. Sexier. He smiled at me before answering, knowing exactly what I was thinking.

"Come here. Lie beside me," he motioned with an outstretched arm. I fell into those hands and arms, placing my head on his chest, listening to his heartbeat and his words reverberate throughout his body into my ear. Even then, his chest had grey hair. It never bothered me, not even when I was that young.

"I met her in Castroville, where we grew up. We were high school sweethearts. Married her in front of God and everyone. I said those vows, but what nineteen-year-old boy, yes a boy, really understands that kind of commitment? I didn't. We were very happy that day, but my job soon took me all over the world. It was hard on both of us, and neither of us was mature enough to handle the separation, so we used other people to get back at each other. She eventually found someone who made her happy. I told you a little bit about that. I had to leave. Start over. It was a long time ago, Hannah."

I closed my eyes when he said my name out loud.

"You shouldn't compare yourself to her. You're a very different woman, and I love you for different reasons. I'd like to think I'm a better man than I was right out of high school."

He never told me her name, and I never asked him about her again. That was forty-eight years ago, but there were times during our marriage I felt her ghost, the first wife married in a church. It could have been because I never had a first love, someone in the innocence of my youth I dreamed of marrying, raising a family alongside my high school girlfriends. All the things so normal in a small town. But I was different from the Junction girls, just like the women I met in Rocksprings. My love story began with an older man, a divorced Catholic, with money. Those choices I made were taboo for a young woman from a small town in Texas. Plus, we had the audacity to sit in the same pew at St. Mary's in Rocksprings with women and men who never broke the sacrament of marriage. The Church didn't recognize us as married, along with the rest of the parishioners, until August made enough cash contributions. We were the talk of the town, no doubt about it!

People might have marked me early on as "one of those women," never to be confused as a local gal, but at least in central Texas they'd never be rude to me in public. After all, it wasn't ladylike. I'd never be one of the girls, but civility in a small town had its understood protocol.

So they showed their gentility to me and August by delivering the occasional invitation to a social event or a phone call requesting how we were getting along. When August died, their gentility was delivered by casserole dishes, funeral sprays, and sympathy cards with praying hands and white crosses. There'd be plenty of time for me to return what was expected by writing thank you cards to them, the final act in the social rituals of a small town. But today I wasn't doing it. Etiquette standards gave me a week or two. Yes, it was all part of what we expected from ourselves and others in the game of life.

I returned to filling the empty cup of loneliness by remembering him and our honeymoon in France. As I sat on the living room floor with his mother's antique shipping trunk opened, photo albums, dried flower buds, and restaurant menus recorded our life as husband and wife.

The first photo was of us standing in front of Les Deux Magots, the famous café in the Saint-Germain-des-Prés district, where the literary and intellectual greats of the Lost Generation of writers met for conversation and drink in the twenties. I listened for the voices of F. Scott Fitzgerald, Ernest Hemingway, and Ezra Pound, as they sat among their peers, openly discussing what was very much taboo in America.

I imagined a young and cynical Hemingway alone at a table, smoking, drinking a whiskey, drafting a scene for *The Sun Also Rises*, while his first wife, the favorite wife in retrospect, sat alone in a dark apartment with an infant son and a cat. Hadley, ever the supportive wife, was soon replaced. Here it was again, the oldest story in the world of the dutiful first wife replaced by a younger second wife. Poor Hadley, older and unassuming, sacrificed all in the name of Art.

As I stared at the picture, remembering those authors who lived the decadence and passion of the Roaring Twenties in Paris, I thought of the opening line to Charles Dickens's *Tale of Two Cities*, "It was the best of times, it was the worst of times, it was the age of wisdom, it was the age of foolishness, it was the epoch of belief, it was the epoch of incredulity, it was the season of Light, it was the season of Darkness, it was the spring of hope, it was the winter of despair, we had everything . . . "

True, no artist in 1920s Paris lost a head to a guillotine like in Dickens's novel, set during the French Revolution, yet their lives were severed by booze and insanity. There were winners and losers, depending on where fate threw you. For the wives, it was never a happy ending.

Christened as the original flapper by her author husband, F. Scott Fitzgerald, Zelda, the lively American girl in Paris, died in a fire in a mental hospital in North Carolina. Fitzgerald drank himself to death in Hollywood. Hemingway burned through marriages until blowing his brains out. My grandmother would have dismissed the Lost Generation as aptly named, in need of prayer. But my grandmother's words could also be much harsher. She had little patience for careless people. Being carefree was a privilege of the rich, something she never knew as a girl, much less as a woman without education or money in central Texas.

Grandma Schoen was never anyone's fool. She would have looked directly at Hemingway, meeting the intensity of his blue eyes with the clear blue of hers and said, "You've made your bed, now lie in it."

I remember when my brother Buddy was running wild with women during his rodeo days, she confronted him at the Sunday dinner table with, "You sleep with dogs, you'll wind up with fleas, too." Buddy laughed at her, but I was embarrassed for both of them.

I couldn't imagine her dancing on top of a Paris cabaret table like Zelda, no more than I could imagine her sacrificing all for Art. That generation of Texas women sacrificed for their children and did what their husbands told them to do. It was a man's world, where women didn't drive, talk back, or give opinions. My grandpa was no exception. For Albert Schoen, a liberated woman was not "ladylike" and considered to be on the same path as the legendary Jezebel, who met her death by being pitched out the window; her lifeless body eaten by wild dogs below.

I weighed every difference between Paris and Junction, Texas, as I sat in the restaurant, looking at the two life-sized Chinese figures hanging on the wall near our table. In Paris, passion made life worth living, no matter what century it happened to be.

"That is love, to give away everything, to sacrifice everything, without the slightest desire to get anything in return," said Albert Camus, as noted on the back of the menu the waiter handed me in the restaurant.

I studied it closely, growing more and more anxious, wondering how to pronounce entrées, wondering what the entrée was made of, beef, chicken, frog. . . . When August felt my tension, he put his hand over mine.

"Let me order for us, Hannah. I promise you'll love it. Trust me?"

"Thank you," I replied, feeling my face flush with embarrassment.

We dined on duck foie gras with poilâne, served with a rich and deep Bordeaux that created a warmth inside me so that I never, ever wanted to leave this restaurant, or the man sitting directly in front of me. Although I had eaten duck before, in a gumbo made by my fun-loving aunt from Louisiana, the spices of duck foie gras didn't overwhelm the senses as cayenne pepper and Tabasco did in a gumbo. I smiled thinking of my Aunt Rita, knowing she was probably laughing at me from heaven, wishing she could help me with the French pronunciation of the dishes served.

August and I lingered over the wine and food, talking about the Lost Generation writers from America who ate in this restaurant fifty years ago. August looked at his watch, announced it was three p.m., and motioned for the waiter to bring the check. I learned much later, three p.m. was the understood time for lovers in Paris, an afternoon interlude for women and men. We took a cab back to the hotel and made love until the evening street lights appeared outside our window.

————

The light changed in the living room bay windows as the sun began to go down on this day. I got up and turned the lights on, leaving the photo albums and the memories there on the floor, in disarray. After taking Abby out, I fried two eggs for supper, but I left half of it on my plate. I just didn't feel like eating, so Abby had eggs for supper, too.

Looking out the kitchen widow, I thought I saw August walking from the barn to the south pasture. He was wearing the all-weather vest I bought him several years ago for Christmas. His hat was pulled low over his brow. But it wasn't him, only my heart wanting to convince my head he wasn't gone.

That night I talked to him in our bed. I did this every night since he died. I truly believed he could hear me. Since I was a child, my mother and grandmother told me the dead became our guardian angels, helping us on earth. Maybe our loved ones who leave this life too early know our pain at being left behind, the hardship of walking this earth without them. I had no problem believing August was still helping me, guiding me through my life. I could feel him all around me.

I wasn't in bed for more than ten minutes or so when I heard the sound of coyotes close to the house. Shrill cries, followed by intense barking. It was always bone chilling, no matter how many times in my life I've heard it. It's a sound a human never gets used to, because it's the arrogant noise of cowardly predators moving in a pack, celebrating the death of its prey, a prey alone and smaller in size. I've hated coyotes since I could remember.

It wasn't uncommon in the Hill Country to see forty or more carcasses of coyotes hanging from fence posts along the property line of a ranch. Some say the bounty hunters were showing off their skill, just like gun fighters from the Old West placing notches on their gun handles for every man they killed. It was also a way of lining up their paid work, for each pelt they displayed was cash money.

I remember Joseph collecting ears of dead coyotes when Edwards County offered cash money for its predator management program a few years ago. I watched him slice off those velvety ears from the carcasses on the fence line at our place with a hunting knife he kept in his right boot. I guess it was easier showing a body part as evidence of the kill rather than the entire body. It was a gruesome sight, even for me, a woman who spent her entire life on the land.

The coyote was a hated animal, and a reminder to me that life on this ranch was a thin line between prey and predator. I wasn't in France with the love of my life. I was alone on a 640-acre working ranch between central and West Texas, where the land was just as hard and mean as the predators lurking in the shadows waiting for the next easy kill.

August, stay with me until I fall asleep and in all my dreams tonight. I'm feeling afraid. Don't know if I have the stamina to stay out here alone. I've loved this land, walking it every day with you. I feel like I'd lose a part of myself if I sold it. I know I'd lose you. All the memories would up and disappear. You were a tender man, although you never let many people close to you, mostly just me and Sam. Those early months, after he was born, you'd bring him to our bed, tucking him in next to me so I could nurse him. Soon, you'd both be asleep. I'd reach across you and turn out the light, lying in bed in the dark, thinking of our little family, wanting to be pregnant again. We hoped for a daughter after Sam was born, but that dream never came true for us.

CHAPTER ELEVEN

Ariela

Northeastern Coahuila, Mexico

The headlights lit a small path in front of the truck, while all around it, the desert and sky were one, a blackness that went on for miles and miles, whispering to me. I was powerless against it, against the two boys in the front seat. Katia's head lay in my lap as she whimpered in her sleep. But I didn't sleep. I never closed my eyes; instead I rested them on the back of Aamon's head. Then quietly, I repositioned my body, so I could get a side glance of him. He was slumped over in the passenger seat, asleep, with the belt still wrapped around his hand, ready to use its big buckle on Katia again.

She made the mistake of fighting with them, just as we drove past the last few houses of Zaragoza, already a mile or so from the nail salon.

"You take us home, Ricky. You promised us a mani-pedi. That's why we got into this truck. You and your ugly friend aren't getting nothing off us."

Her shouts were returned with laughter from Ricky, then I heard a belt buckle rattle in the front seat, while both of Ricky's hands remained on the steering wheel. Aamon whipped her with the buckle, holding the leather tails of it, doubled up in one fist. He grabbed her by the hair, pulling her closer to him, when she tried to hide on the floorboard.

"Don't touch her face, man. Be careful," Ricky shouted.

The blows of the buckle came harder and faster on her stomach, shoulders, and thighs. Then exhaustion overtook him, between the panting and cursing of each blow. Finally, he stopped. I opened my eyes then. I wanted to fight Aamon, pull the belt out of his fist and beat him with it, but I knew it would only make it worse for us. Ricky would have stopped the truck and beat us alongside Aamon. Still, I hated myself for not helping her.

53

Katia retreated to the right side of the truck where I sat, curling herself upon me like a little dog. I rubbed the rising welts on her bare thighs, stroked her hair, and rocked her back and forth, against the seat, until she fell asleep. Now, hours had passed outside the windows of the truck. Hours I stroked her hair, my tears falling onto the long black tresses. I thought of my mother and father, worried, wondering where I was. Maybe I'd never see them again. Maybe Ricky and his friend would kill us and bury us in the desert, like we were nobodies, left in the middle of nowhere, along the side of the road.

"Wake up," Ricky yelled, bringing the truck to a stop. "Tomas is already here. Bastardo loco, just as soon cut your throat as talk to you. Aamon, man, listen to me. You got to let him be the boss. He's not going to like you've already marked one up. Keep your mouth shut. Let me talk to him."

Aamon opened the truck door I was leaning against. He grabbed my hands and bound them in a plastic tie wrap, then stood me up against the truck. Next was Katia. She didn't fight him. She didn't even look at him. I knew then Aamon broke her spirit with the belt buckle. We walked between the two boys toward a little house. It was a small shack, something hunters would use during deer season. Before we got to the door, a large man, taller than both Aamon and Ricky, opened the door.

"You're late," the man said, opening the door wider. On a table behind him was a kerosene lamp, shining on his face and clothes. He was about the age of Papá, maybe a little younger. He wore his black hair in a big fat ponytail. Looked like a bird could live in it, it was so bushy, probably full of knots. Just like Aamon and Ricky, he wore expensive cowboy boots on his feet. Those two were quiet in front of him. I looked at their faces while the boss was talking. Aamon never looked up at him. Ricky just nodded his head.

"Put them in there. I'll look at them in the morning," the boss man said, then sat down near the kerosene lamp.

Aamon pushed me and Katia toward a closed door. He opened it, shoved us in, and slammed it closed. A small slit of light from the closed door spilled onto the floor. Three mattresses were pushed to different sides of the room with a white bucket near the boarded window. The smell of caca and pee and the whimpering of the three other girls in the room made

Katia cry. I wasn't going to cry. I couldn't. All I could do was think of my family, how worried they must be. It was all my fault. I should have never got into the truck. Just gone home to my family, but I didn't.

"Hush, Katia. You don't want them coming in here."

"I just wanted to have some fun. That's all, have a laugh or two with Ricky. Look at where it got us. We got to get out of here, run away. Maybe not tonight. I'm tired. So hungry. Don't hate me, Ariela. You're all I got. My daddy, dead. Mama won't come looking for me. Nobody cares if I'm gone. I'm one less mouth to feed."

"Quiet, now. We'll get away tomorrow. Just sleep."

We lay close to the sides of the mattress, far away from the stains in the middle. She cried herself to sleep, but I didn't. All night I listened to the men talking outside the door, the girls breathing and whimpering in their sleep. Outside, I heard dogs scratching and barking near the boarded window. Morning came when Tomas opened the door. Every creature within a hundred miles shook within their bones, wondering what the day would bring from the boss man.

Five girls, some even younger than me, cowered on the mattresses, waiting for him to speak. The federales wouldn't come to save us. We were by the thousands all along the Texas and Mexico border. Who could decide which one to save? No one, so our deaths became as unimportant as the lives we lived on the wrong side of the border.

"I own your body," he whispered, then repeated a little louder. "Comprende?"

I felt a rush of water near me, then realized Katia peed on herself. I covered it up on the mattress by sitting on the little puddle, hoping he wouldn't see it.

"Your bodies are mine. I don't care what you think or want. I own you. You two, come here."

He pointed to me and Katia. I got up first, then reached down to help Katia. We stood in front of him with our heads lowered.

He looked us over slowly. No expression, ignoring the pee stain over the front and back of our jeans. He then reached out and touched a welt on Katia's throat.

"Aamon and his magic trick."

He pushed us through the open door.

"Aamon, feed them, but don't lay another hand on them or I'll cut and bleed you out here. I'm taking them to Houston. Got a customer coming in for the NBA play-offs, needs to do some entertaining for his clients. *Mucho dinero en Houston.* You and Ricky, take the others to El Paso. Different market. Soldiers in El Paso, Fort Bliss, don't care too much about looks, as long as it's cheap."

CHAPTER TWELVE

Hannah
Durand Ranch

I woke to the sound of a barn owl outside my window the morning of the tornado anniversary. The church's anniversary Mass was this evening. I should go, but I could think of a million reasons why I didn't want to. Watching the bird take flight, his eerie shriek trailing behind him, I wondered if he was the same owl August said nested in the oak near the deer blind on the north side of the ranch.

The morning call to my brother Buddy was a reminder of today's date and the three months I've been a widow. The ache of it and all it encompassed was the same as the day August died, but I kept pushing myself, thinking I had to see people, go to town, improve the ranch. I had come to the realization there was no real reason I should still be alive. August was gone. My son was a grown man. He and his family had their own lives. The grief wouldn't subside, and I refused to burden other people with it.

My brothers had their own problems with their families. Even Buddy had slowed down since losing Alice, plus it wasn't an easy thing for a man that age to drive all the way out to the ranch, just to keep me company.

Family wasn't what it was when I was growing up. People today didn't want more stress in their lives, and that's what I was, a responsibility to my son and an obligation to my daughter-in-law. My grandsons no longer enjoyed coming to the ranch as much as they did when August was alive. Their weekend visit at Easter was cut short by the blunt reminder life was fragile out here. You had to pay attention to everything you did when walking out on the land. It was an important lesson August gave to Sam, but Sam didn't teach his children nearly as well.

Aaron and Will had set out for a walk after breakfast with their dog, Bandit, an undisciplined, nervous beagle. Early spring was a tender time on the ranch. Fawns were learning to walk, quail and turkey were born, the natural world was awakening from winter. It was a rite of passage I held sacred, protecting the newly born in their vulnerability. I almost walked with the boys that day, but I held back, thinking I shouldn't interfere with their freedom to roam the land by themselves. I also wanted them to know I trusted them to make the right decisions in the event of something happening out here, without an adult constantly looking over their shoulders. The one I didn't trust was Bandit. He was a reckless animal, and my grandsons, as hard as it was to admit, weren't taught to respect wildlife like they should have been, by either parent. I didn't want to make any trouble, especially with Leslie. I knew she wanted to be anywhere else but here for the weekend.

The boys weren't gone but about an hour, when Will burst into the kitchen with tears running down his red, sweaty face.

"Grandma, Bandit chased a fawn and its mother. The doe got away, but Bandit caught up to the fawn, biting it on the neck and legs. I screamed at Aaron to help me stop Bandit. He just stood there. I had to grab Bandit with both hands around his neck and throw him off the fawn. It was bleeding everywhere and crying for its mother. I didn't know what to do. Aaron said to leave it, its mother would come looking for it."

"Where's your brother?" Sam asked, standing up from the kitchen table.

"He's outside with Bandit."

I reached out to hug Will. He had always been a more sensitive, loving child than Aaron. Aaron was Leslie, through and through.

"It's okay, honey. The mother will come for her baby. They're probably together this very moment. I'm sure she was watching y'all from a safe distance until she could get to her baby. Things happen quickly out on the land. You have to pay close attention."

"You and your brother are at the point you don't know the difference between reality and a video game. You can't mess around on the ranch. There's the predator and the prey. Life and death. A split second can change the two out here," Sam shouted at the boys.

"That's a bit dramatic don't you think, Sam?" Leslie said, standing in the doorway of the kitchen.

She didn't wait for an answer, and the three of us followed the sound of the front door slamming behind her. Sam looked at me, and I turned away, sick to my stomach. I didn't let Will see my face. He was an innocent who didn't understand the violence of a sudden death, but he was quickly learning.

A few weeks later I stared into the morning light of five a.m., hoping to see the owl outside my window. There he was, nestled in the oak August and I planted the first year we were married. He returned my stare, frightening, direct eye contact, then twisting his neck, he screeched at me before taking flight again. Owls were strange birds.

While the tornado Mass was set for six p.m., I wanted to get there earlier and light a candle for those poor souls killed, seventy-five of them, on that fateful day in April 1927. After that tornado, only eight buildings remained in Rocksprings. The telephone operator had to go out of town to find a live telephone line to get help. People from all over the area, even Mexico, came to help. The first responders were soldiers on horseback from Fort Clark. To this day, it remained one of Texas's deadliest tornadoes.

There was another bad tornado during the early nineties. It didn't have the death toll of the 1927 storm, but several townspeople were killed; families I knew from church, even young women and children. There was quite a bit of destruction to homes and businesses. Some of those homes still haven't been rebuilt. It broke my heart to drive through town and see the slabs where once a family home stood.

The tornado also destroyed the high school gym. August donated a lot of money to its rebuilding, just like he did to other buildings and causes in Rocksprings, although you'd never see his name on a plaque or his picture in the *Mohair Weekly*.

I'd better start moving if I wanted to bring something to the Sacred Heart potluck, following Mass. There was a chicken in the freezer for a casserole without me going into town to buy groceries, so I put it in the sink for defrosting when I heard the rumble of thunder in the distance. An hour later, a violent thunderstorm moved across the land, with lightning striking the barn. Maybe Sam was right. I needed to sell this place and move into town. If that barn had caught on fire, I'd never have the strength to put it out. I'd just have to watch it burn to the ground.

It wasn't unusual to have thunderstorms in early April. I've marked my entire life on this ranch watching animals and the changing of seasons. It wouldn't be an easy thing to give up. Spring brought the black buck, white tail, and sika, along with the occasional sighting of turkeys or an aged buck.

The aged animals died with dignity here. So unlike humans, wasting away in a hospital or nursing home. All shipped away due to their inability to contribute or take care of themselves. I watched many old bucks stumble across the land in their last few months, their movement whispering to the others that they would no longer run following the next full moon. They would simply die where they had lived their entire lives.

———————

"How you getting along out there, Hannah?"

Joseph was always the first to welcome me. It didn't matter if it was at the grocery store or church. He'd been doing that since he was a kid. I didn't know if he felt sorry for me because he knew how women talked about me. As if at this age I'd be a threat, taking someone's husband, but I'd noticed since August's passing, most of the couple friends we knew didn't invite me to join them any longer. The emails and phone calls began dying off until they stopped completely. No card parties or dinners in town would be coming my way from them. I was a single woman, now. I belonged in a different group.

"Joseph, come out and see the garden you started. Don't wait until the summer heat kills off the tomatoes."

His wife Elizabeth, his daughters, and their families sitting next to him shot me a look. Every one of them, so I knew what they thought of me. I ignored them.

"Come get some for pico or salsa."

He smiled his careful, slow smile. That same smile I've witnessed for decades out on the ranch, through all the seasons I had known him. He was aging well, still a muscular man from all the physical labor on the ranch, but grey streaked through his black hair. Deep lines crossed his forehead and in the corner of his eyes when he spoke.

"I'll stop by next week. I need to check the fencing on the west end of the ranch. We'll also need to talk about a new pump for the water trough."

It's been on its last legs for a few years now. There's a new piston pump, like the old-fashioned hand pump. This pump lets the cattle push a lever with their noses to activate the water. Saves a lot of money and water."

"Good, Joseph."

I saw the altar boys lining up at the back of the church, so I took a seat several pews away from Joseph and his family. I'm sure Elizabeth appreciated that.

Following Mass, dinner was served in the church hall. It was a beautiful reminder of how much I missed eating with others. The sound of children running through the hall and people talking and laughing made for the best meal I'd had in months. Most of my meals were standing at the kitchen sink, eating a piece of toast while staring out the window. While I hated driving at night—it seemed like my eyes got worse each year—the company was worth it. I needed people; I needed the sound of life in my daily routine. Never thought I'd admit that, but since August died, I'd been feeling very alone in this old world.

I stopped at the dollar store on the way home from church for a new rawhide chew for Abby and creamer for morning coffee. This was where most residents of Rocksprings shopped. In fact, it was such a popular choice Rocksprings had two dollar stores, odd staples of the changing times in this town, where empty storefronts populated most of downtown.

Poverty and the lack of jobs had most families eating cheap canned vegetables and potted meat available at the dollar stores. It was a sobering fact to realize this was one of the best jobs in town. At least you got a steady paycheck. The local grocery store employed mostly high school kids to stock shelves. The adults working as checkers were lucky to get twenty hours a week.

I wasn't in there but a few minutes until I walked out the door, realizing it was dark and I'd have a hard time getting back to the ranch. There wasn't a full moon, and those gravel roads were hard to navigate in the dark, even without the fear of a deer running in front of me, hitting the truck or going through the windshield.

I drove past the site where Antonio Rodríguez was burned alive in 1910 after being accused of murdering a white woman at her ranch outside of Rocksprings. The twenty-year-old ranch hand from Las Vascas, Mexico, was put in the Rocksprings jail. The next day a mob stormed the jail, removed the young Mexican from the iron bars keeping him safe, tied him to a wooden stake, and burned him alive. His murder created outrage in Mexico, followed by riots in Mexico City. Skirmishes occurred between Anglos and Mexicans at the border, with heated diplomatic talks between the United States and Mexico.

The horror of racism and the violence it spewed on a cold day in November 1910 never left Rocksprings. People still talked about it; some with shame, others with a sense of pride. I made the sign of the cross and said a prayer for Antonio Rodríguez's soul every time I drove past that site. He never got the chance to tell his story in a courtroom, because of the color of his skin.

Once I drove out of the city limits, the night was deep, bottomless without the artificial lights of a small town. I could barely see my hand in front of me, so I kept the speed at fifty on the farm-to-market road, then dropped to forty once the asphalt became gravel near the ranch gate. It would be all right, I kept telling myself. There wasn't any traffic out here. If there was at this time of night, someone was either lost or up to something.

CHAPTER THIRTEEN

Ariela

Northern Mexico into West and Central Texas

I saw the boss man remove the Mexico license plate and exchange it for two from Texas when I looked through the little window not far from the table Katia and I sat at, eating cold tortillas, washing it down with bottled water. Next to that car were all the trucks the other men drove, bringing girls just like me and Katia to this horrible place. There were too many of them for us to run away once we got outside again. We'd just be running into the desert until we dropped; then they would come in their trucks to get us, two brown-skinned girls against the pale ocean of the desert, such easy targets to find.

The boss man's four-door car with the Texas plates was older than all the trucks, nothing fancy like Ricky's truck. No fancy wheels or paint job; the car looked like something an old granny would drive. The boss man opened the trunk of the car and came back in the house. The trunk just stayed like that; no one shut it or carried anything from the house to put in it. It stayed open until Ricky wrapped duct tape around our mouths, pulling our hair into the sticky adhesive, whispering to us to keep quiet though he never looked us in the face. He bound our hands in the plastic tie wrap, again, then like discarded, dirty spoons, put us in the trunk, side by side. Ricky, a boy I went to grade school with, treated me like that, like I was nothing, *la basura*, trash you burn at the dump. I guess he thought whispering instead of screaming to keep quiet was the only respect we deserved. He was one of them, a gang member. I was stupid to think he would treat us differently just because we knew him all those years ago when he was still a shy, sad boy.

The tiny light I saw from inside the trunk was shaped like a thin rectangle missing one side. Without being able to see, I lost my sense of time and direction. The only routine I could keep so I could control my fear was counting every beat of Katia's heart pounding in my ear. I knew if I ran out of numbers, we were out of Mexico and out of luck.

"Same place I always cross over, man. Del Rio. They know me and the car. Then Highway 55 to Uvalde, ending south of Sonora. Quicker to get I-10 from Junction, but border patrol was all over the place since the raid in September. There's a motel in Rocksprings. I'll make my calls from there. Get them cleaned up, fed. Got some people to see in San Antonio, who will get them clothes, makeup, before dropping them off in Houston to the manager. Back here in a week. You bring all the money from El Paso here, Ricky. I know what you'll make. Just like Phoenix. Same market, man."

"I'd never cheat you, Tomas."

"Liar. You'd cheat your mother if she had anything worth stealing."

The car started, and the sound of gravel from the road pounded in our ears as sweat, salty and wet, dripped from our noses, thighs, our body smells sickening in the tiny space of the trunk. I wanted to tell Katia we could escape when we got to the motel in Texas, but my lips were pulled tight like a single thread sewed by the tape covering it. The only hope I could give her was rocking just a little against her body, reminding her I was still with her. She was not alone. I knew she was crying, though I couldn't see her face. I felt the vibration of her body, along with the rocks on the road. Hours and hours of this. I wondered why I was being the stronger one, when all the years I'd known her, she was the leader, and I was the follower.

I knew none of the places the boss man spoke of except San Antonio and Houston. I knew people who made it to those cities got good jobs, some sending money home to parents, even bringing their brothers and sisters to live with them in Texas. A lot of people spoke Spanish in Houston and San Antonio. We could get help there, but I didn't know how far it was from this motel in Rocksprings the demon mentioned. Maybe we could walk to San Antonio from there. I just wanted to go home and tell my papá and mama I was sorry for making them worry. I was sorry for not listening, sorry for getting in a truck with evil boys, but all I'd thought about was getting my nails done. How pretty my hands would be! What color to pick? Purple, silver, red. I didn't listen to those boys with my head.

I listened to my own wants and climbed into the truck right after Katia did. She was the leader, and I was a follower.

When I woke up again, there was no longer the slant of light coming from outside the trunk. I couldn't hear the gravel underneath me; the road was smooth. The only sounds were the panted breathing of Katia and the whine of the car wheels beneath us. I was glad she wasn't crying anymore. I could take the heat and thirst more than I could her crying. I just couldn't allow myself to think like she did. She knew what was coming. That demon driving the car would probably rape us as soon as we got to the motel, somewhere in Texas, somewhere in the town called Rocksprings, where no one knew or cared for us. We were poor Mexican girls crossing the border, illegals and wetbacks to everyone on this side. But at home, I was someone's daughter and sister. At home, people knew my name and loved me. Katia had none of this. It was buried with her father.

The car finally stopped. It was night somewhere in Texas. I could hear crickets and the sound of air conditioners humming in windows. Then, the car door slammed, and I followed the sound of the demon's boots walking away from us, then the opening of a door, followed by the sound of a little bell.

Katia began rocking back and forth, faster and faster, slamming against me. Maybe she was trying to escape from the trunk, hoping the friction would break the tie wraps around our wrists and ankles. She knew she wasn't strong enough to make that happen, but she kept rocking, faster and faster against me. I heard the demon's boots approaching the car. His fist came down hard on the trunk panel. Katia stopped rocking.

He drove the car a short distance, maybe a few yards, then stopped.

"I'm going to open the trunk and let you out. If you fight me, I'll kill you. I'll dump both of your bodies in the Devil's Sink Hole, just north of here," he said from the inside of the car.

Then I heard him light a cigarette, followed by the heavy exhale of its smoke. "Do you know what the Devil's Sink Hole is, chicas? It's where I throw the bodies of girls who don't listen. You can't climb out of the hole, even if you're still alive when I throw you in. Some say it's the biggest cave in Texas, and we know how everything is bigger in Tejas! But even better than its size is the millions of bats rising from its opening every night. The Devil's Sink Hole! The gringos got something right in naming it. I call it a mass grave for girls who don't respect me. Easier for me, too. I don't need a shovel to bury you."

The next sound I heard was the car door opening, then the crunch of his boots walking on gravel. He touched the trunk, and it opened. He pulled Katia out first and closed the trunk again. Silence for just a minute or two, then he came back for me. I tried hard to see where I was, but after being in that trunk so long and without water, I didn't trust my eyes. He opened the door to a little cinder block room, all in a row, lots of cinder block rooms, so maybe this was a motel, and we were in Rocksprings, the place those men talked about earlier.

I looked across the room quickly and saw Katia on one of the two beds. Her wrists and ankles were still bound. Her hair and eyes were wild. The demon pushed me onto the other bed, opposite Katia's. Sweating and breathless, he then went back out to the car, returning with a bottle of tequila. Standing in front of the two beds, he drank from the bottle, eyeing both of us, until there was nothing left to drink, and nothing left in his brain.

He bent down and removed a long, curved knife from one of his boots, then stepped toward the bed Katia was in; leaning over, he placed the tip of the knife to her throat.

"You try to run away, I'll cut your throat. Leave you to bleed to death on the bed. Then off to the Devil's Sink Hole we go." He then turned towards me, "You listening?" He pointed the knife at me, and I shook my head yes.

He cut the tie wraps, then lit a cigarette, still watching both of us as he stood in front of the two beds. Then he walked outside, closing the door behind him. I flew to Katia's side. She began to cry, trying to speak to me through the duct tape, her hair tangled in it.

Our eyes met again, and I knew what she was trying to tell me. She had given up. *"Goodbye, Ariela. Forgive me, love me, don't leave me."* Then she curled herself into a ball and began the same rocking motion again.

I kissed her wild eyes, then curled my body around her as a shield. Inside me I chanted the Hail Mary prayer over and over again, sometimes saying Mama's name out loud, then Papá's, until I heard the sound of the key in the motel door.

The demon walked toward us, separating our bodies to the two different beds. He then leaned over Katia, pulling her hair with one fist until she uncurled the ball she made of her body. I watched him tear her clothes off, her dirty jeans, her little panties soiled from the days in the car, then he lay on top of her. I closed my eyes, but I could not close my ears. I prayed inside me, stronger and stronger, calling on saints and angels to rescue us. *Please Guardian Angel, take our hands and fly us home, home to Mexico, to our little houses with our families.* But no angel came for us.

He was done with her, and I was next, but just as quickly as we got into the truck with Ricky and Aamon and left Zaragoza, the weeping of Katia was replaced by the demon's scream. She had kicked him between the legs when he moved off her. Her hundred pounds of flesh and blood hurt him.

I watched him move the knife across her little throat, breaking her St. Michael medal and the chain it danced upon. It sailed from her throat and landed next to me on the bed. With her last heartbeat, she became the leader, again. I followed, meeting her eyes. Those eyes told me to run.

I did, through the unlocked motel door, out into the Texas night, as black as the soul of the demon chasing me. I ran as fast as I could from the demon and the Devil's Sink Hole.

CHAPTER FOURTEEN

Ariela

Rocksprings, Texas

I let the last image of Katia, her brown eyes focused somewhere between heaven and hell, burn into my soul as I ran barefoot out of the motel parking lot. I ran like the devil was chasing me, because he was. I turned around one time, where the parking lot met the wider street of the town, and looked at him. Beneath the outdoor light of the motel room, I saw him struggling to get his pants on, cursing me with every breath he took. His hair loose and wild. The door to the motel room was wide open, like a person's mouth in shock. Inside was the lifeless, naked body of Katia and the blood-filled mattress beneath her.

I didn't scream, I knew better. If anybody else heard that scream, they weren't going to poke their heads out and rescue me. Like me, they knew better. The rows of closed motel doors in front of me remained closed. The only sound came from the demon.

"You can't run from me. I know where your mother is, your sister, *tu padre*, stupid girl," he laughed, leaning against the door of the motel room, as he pushed a foot into a boot.

His threat made me stop running. Would he kill my family if I didn't go back? He'd kill me anyway, or sell me to someone who'd kill me. I continued to stare at him as he pulled his cell phone out of the back pocket of his jeans.

"I'm in Rocksprings, Tejas, Miguel. One dead, the other escaped. When I get her, I'll call you."

When he said that, our eyes locked. I ran across the main street, from the motel parking lot, with little pebbles embedded in my bare feet. I ran until I heard his car start, then I hid behind a little house off the main road.

It was there I heard a voice call out to me, along with the sound of a dog barking.

"Ariela, come home, *mi hija*. *Prisa*, quickly, we're all waiting."

The voice sounded like my mother. *Mi Mama!* Then the smell of roses surrounded me. A goodness like home ran through my body, as if I just woke up from my bed in Zaragoza with little Alicia, my sister, beside me. And together, we joined my brother, Mama and Papá, at the little wooden table in the kitchen, eating a breakfast of eggs and tortillas. Those visions of my family made today, the past week, nothing more than a bad dream I would soon wake from, but no matter how hard I tried, I never woke up from this nightmare. Maybe I was imagining the voice. My stomach was twisted in knots from not eating in two days. The area between my legs was raw from peeing on myself. I was sick and hungry. Maybe my mind was gone, too.

I didn't want to cry. I couldn't cry. I had to think about getting home. I heard the voice again. Maybe it was the voice of a mother, in the darkness, calling for her daughter who hadn't obeyed her and wandered off, getting lost. She was guiding her home with her voice. Maybe it was the voice of a woman, *mujer extraditonaria*, kind and good, who only wanted to help me find my way home.

I was lost in the dark. In this town. In this country. I didn't know the language, the people, but maybe, maybe I'd hear the voice again, and it would tell me the way home.

The voice called out, "Ariela," and I followed, running farther and farther away from the demon. When I got tired of running, I concentrated on Katia, her large, brown eyes staring at me. I could run forever if I stayed focused on her. She died so I could live. Now, I had to stay alive to tell her story. I had to let her mother know what happened to her little girl.

I ran behind the houses and stores along the main road in town for a long time, hiding behind the bright lights and people moving in and out of shops. The sounds of families talking and babies crying haunted me. I wanted to ask for help, but I was afraid. I only heard English and saw white people. I could only imagine what I looked like if I showed myself to them, so I ran past the school, then toward the church with its lights on, with Jesus and angels staring back at me in the stained-glass windows.

I hid behind a shed in the back of the church and held my side. It hurt, hurt so much. I didn't think I could go on, but then the voice and the dog's barking returned. I followed those sounds, holding my side, sticking to the shadows in the ditches along the bigger road, outside of town.

I was an illegal immigrant, and the border patrol would lock me up if they found me. I didn't know for how long, maybe for months. We heard those stories back in Zaragoza, how families were separated for months; even little babies were taken from their mothers, all the little ones together in a cage with one or two strangers to care for them. Who would wipe away the hundreds and hundreds of tears from motherless babies? No one.

I'd keep walking until I found a Mexican who shared my language. She would know my worry. She would help me get home to Zaragoza and my family. Then I could see Katia's mother and tell her how her daughter saved me.

I walked, still with the sound of the dog barking in the distance. At times I thought the dog was walking alongside me. I sat down on the road to rest for a minute, and the voice of the woman spoke. Followed by the smell of roses, many roses, as if I were in a beautiful garden of roses without a care in the world.

"Ariela, the name I chose for you means lioness of God. *Querida una*, listen to me, you are stronger than you know."

"Mama, help me. I'm sorry I made you worry. I want to come home with you." I reached my arms out into the darkness, hoping to touch her.

"I'll never leave your side, daughter."

The voice was gone. The roses were gone. The dog no longer barked. Abandoned, my feet bleeding, tired beyond anything I had ever known, I lay in the ditch along the road and curled into the smallest ball I could, hoping to disappear, so no one would find and hurt me.

CHAPTER FIFTEEN

Hannah

Rocksprings, Texas

A late model sedan was following me closely as I drove back to the ranch after stopping at the dollar store. Its headlights flooded the cabin of my truck, often blinding me, making me a nervous wreck. Although I was unsure of the shoulder, I decided to pull over and let the car pass. When I looked back in my review mirror, the headlights were gone. I slowed down to about five mph, thinking the car was trying to pass me, but I still didn't see anything. It was then I heard the dog barking. I drove along at that same slow speed, hoping I wouldn't hit the dog. When the barking continued, I stopped the truck. Craning my neck to get as close as I could to the windshield, the two beams from the headlights revealed nothing was in front of me. The barking continued, so I grabbed the flashlight stashed between the seats, got out of the truck, and called for the dog.

"Come on, boy. Good dog, come here."

The whole time I was praying I hadn't hit one of the neighbor's dogs. I continued to walk in the path of the headlights, and the sound of the dog until I saw them. In a drainage ditch on the side of the road was a hunched figure of a human, with a dog standing over the body.

Merciful God.

I continued calling to the dog, gray in the headlights, long haired, maybe one of the blue heelers the ranchers like to keep out here, but I couldn't tell even being this close, so I turned on the flashlight. I could clearly see the hunched figure was a girl, in a fetal position with long, black hair, tangled and knotted. She was barefoot. Her clothes were filthy, with blood on her jeans, near the knees. Probably fell and skinned herself up on the gravel. The smell of urine, feces, and God knows what else was overwhelming, even from this distance.

I walked toward her and the dog, slowly, step by step, afraid the dog would bite me. It was clear the animal was guarding her. For a moment I thought she was a runaway, taking her dog with her for protection. She might be a local teen from a nearby ranching family who fought with her parents over a bad grade or a boyfriend. But the longer I stood over her, I knew this couldn't be true. I could feel it in my gut. Whatever had happened to this girl was evil, and I prayed who or what chased her here wasn't anywhere near.

When I was close enough to touch her and the dog, I lowered my head, my palms open and near my hips, revealing I was no threat to the animal. Just as I reached out to pet the dog, it disappeared. Had I lost my mind? I felt like a stupid old woman who couldn't trust her eyes or mind to see what was in front of her. How could I protect myself or even this girl, passed out on the side of the road? God help me, was she even alive?

She had a pulse. My hand easily wrapped around her wrist, she was that thin, and I'm sure, dehydrated. I followed the headlight beams back to the truck for a jug of water I kept behind the seat next to a clean blanket and a container of hand wipes.

I bent next to her, pushing her hair back from her face, speaking slowly to her about the need to drink water.

"*Quiero ayudarte. Beba un poco de agua.*"

She stirred and slowly opened her eyes. Large, brown eyes full of fear and distrust looked into mine. I cradled her head in my hand and lifted it toward the open container of water. She drank deeply, all the while looking at me, gauging me as either friend or foe. When she was finished, I draped the blanket around her, giving a gentle squeeze to each of her shoulders, assuring her I wouldn't hurt her. It was a warm April night, in the low sixties, but she still shivered under the blanket.

I wanted to see if her bare feet were cut, knowing full well I couldn't carry her back to the truck nor move the truck closer—that would have scared her to death—so I took a few hand wipes to clean her. When I touched her face, she shrank from me. I stopped and looked at her, smiling, making complete eye contact, and whispered, "Amiga."

She looked at the water jug again. I raised her head while she drank. When she finished, I cleaned her face, hands, and feet. I didn't see any additional cuts.

"Mi casa. Vamos."

She nodded, then moved into a squatting position. I linked both hands around her waist and helped her to her feet. Such a tiny girl, she had to be younger than sixteen.

We followed the headlight beams back to the trunk. She stopped once and looked into the sky. A million stars and a quarter moon returned her gaze. I suddenly felt a chill, realizing how alone we were out here. An old woman and a young girl who had suddenly emerged from the gates of hell to here, one of many lone gravel roads that fed off of Highway 377. By what miracle had I found her?

I opened the truck door for her, helping her up, then I covered her with the blanket. She was lying across the bench seat, her hair spilling across it like waves of black ribbon. I slowly drove home, the only place I knew to take her. She'd be safe there until I could call someone for help. Who would I call? The police? Border patrol? Her family? Who was responsible for this girl?

My childhood Spanish, really a mixture of Spanish and English I learned by listening to my neighbors in Junction and Rocksprings, was limited but functional. We were diversified communities before a government agency coined the phrase. Diversity was our shared history and culture, but we also needed each other to survive. This was a harsh land that could rain hail one day and scorch what little vegetation there was the next day.

I laughed at myself for a second. I could hardly believe I got the girl into the truck. Well, my son wouldn't believe it, let alone his wife and kids. My mind and body continued to surprise me. Some days I couldn't remember where I put my glasses, only to find them two hours later on the top of my head. Other days, I was throwing bales of hay from the back of the truck out into the pasture. I felt eighteen again, until I got home and looked in the mirror. Always surprised. Not at the wrinkles and brown spots, but the fact I had become an old woman. I didn't know where all the years went. But tonight, I didn't feel like an old woman; tonight, I was a woman with a purpose in life. Tonight, I felt strong.

She murmured "Mama" at least three times before I got to the first
pasture gate. Before getting out of the truck to open the gate, I placed my
hand on her head for assurance. She released a deep breath but didn't wake
up. I reached underneath the seat and got the flashlight. There was a time I
didn't need that added light to find the latch on the gate.

I listened to the crunch of gravel beneath my boots as I walked toward
the gate, shining the light in front of me. Then I stopped. It sounded like a
car's motor running a few yards behind me. I strained to listen closely, even
stopped walking. Nothing. Then I focused the flashlight in the direction
of the motor running, holding the light steady with both hands, waiting
to see what was in front of me. Nothing. With this night deep and quiet, I
couldn't see my hand in front of me without the flashlight. I stayed in that
position, holding my breath another minute or so, then I walked to the gate
and unlatched it.

Back in the truck, I looked over at the girl asleep on the bench seat
before turning the key over. I drove the truck across the cattle guard, the
sound of each rung as familiar as my heartbeat, then I killed the engine
and reached for the flashlight. I stood in front of the truck, listening, then
I turned the flashlight to view what was behind me. I strained to hear.
Nothing. Still the feeling of being watched, even followed, wouldn't leave
me. The only mistake I've ever made regarding my intuition as a woman
was not trusting it. *Who was out here?*

The sickening taste of fear spread from my gut to every sinew, muscle,
and bone within my body. Only then did I realize who was in my truck.
An illegal. Was there somebody following her? Border patrol? I quickly got
back into the truck and started the engine. I looked down at her, inches
from me, completely vulnerable, half-conscious, and starving. No, it didn't
matter where she was from, or what she was doing here. Beneath the mas-
sive spilled hair and ripped, bloody jeans was a child running for her life.

CHAPTER SIXTEEN

Hannah

Durand Ranch

A bby met us at the door. Poor girl. She wasn't used to being locked up inside the house for this long. She sniffed the feet of the girl as I dragged her across the threshold, still semiconscious, muttering *"Demonio maligno. Salvame,"* each agonizing step I took with her. The pain in my lower back and right shoulder were numbing, but I understood what she was saying, and I knew then we were both in terrible trouble. That poor child had just begged me to save her from an evil demon.

I put her on the couch and covered her with an afghan, then walked back to the front door with Abby.

"Go on, girl," I said, closing the door behind me. I walked with Abby across the porch, then I went back into the house. She'd be gone just long enough for me to give the girl a small bath, maybe even dress her wounds.

I peeked into the living room. She was still asleep, so I headed back into the kitchen, filled a plastic bucket with warm water and body wash. I'd never get her into the bathtub or shower tonight. I hadn't the strength, so a sponge bath would have to do. I gathered a towel, sponge, socks, and nightgown from the back of the house. Just as I was about to enter the living room, I heard Abby barking. She was probably after a raccoon or fox. She'd been inside most of the evening; I'm sure she was enjoying a bit of freedom. I returned to the living room, also dismissing the simple fact the front door was unlocked.

I removed the girl's clothes carefully, the soiled panties, the ripped jeans, the tee shirt with a sparkly unicorn, its single horn of pink glitter flaking off onto the couch when I pulled it above her head.

She was just a little girl, probably weighing no more than a hundred pounds. I removed her bra with a red ribbon and rose emblem between the two small cups. I placed it on the floor next to her other clothes, all childlike in their appearance and size. I'd try to get them all in the washing machine before I went to bed, or else she'd have nothing to wear tomorrow. Maybe she'd be able to wear a little cotton sundress I had. Of course, it would swallow her, but it would be clean, free of the road and all the damage it had done to her.

Placing the towel beneath her, I washed her body, moving the washcloth quickly over her. I didn't want to wake her. It might scare her to death, a stranger washing her. I returned to the kitchen sink to empty the brown water, refilling it with warm suds, scented by a body wash my grandsons gave me for my birthday. The smell of lavender rose from the plastic bucket as I carried it back to the living room. I sat it on the floor next to the couch, placed a towel underneath her bare feet, and knelt next to them, squeezing the sponge with my fist, gently brushing against the cuts and bruises. The many wounds on those tiny feet brought tears to my eyes, thinking how often I gave no thought to the gift of wearing shoes, owning multiple shoes, never once considering what life would be if I had to walk this earth knowing a pair of shoes was a luxury.

I returned to the kitchen sink, rinsing the bucket of its soiled water, then refilling it again with warm, sudsy water. Placing the bucket next to me on the floor, I knelt in front of her feet once more and applied an antibiotic ointment with a Q-tip. Only once did her eyes flutter. I then lavished lotion on both feet, caressing the cracked heels, moving my fingers gently between her toes, desperate to remove the tension from her body while avoiding the open wounds. Then, I covered both feet with a pair of August's cotton socks; their enormous size kept any pressure from being on the cut and bruised feet of this poor girl.

I rinsed her body one more time, moving her into an upright position without awakening her. Now, her body was clean. I smiled, feeling a sense of accomplishment, but more than that, I received the gift of giving to a stranger. Within that tiny moment, we were both safe, and my heart swelled with gratitude for being alive and keeping her alive.

Standing up, I arched my back and stretched, feeling my spine release itself after sitting on the floor. Shaking my hands, I silently demanded my body give me just a bit more strength. I lifted her up, pulled a bunched-up nightgown over her head, then over her body. I stood, stretched my back one more time, and sighed. Feeling bone-weary, I couldn't do anything else tonight, so I placed the afghan over her and turned out the light in the living room.

Walking out onto the porch, I called for Abby. I waited at least ten minutes for her to return, listening to the night sounds of crickets and animals moving through the pasture, the cattle lying low beneath the trees. I whistled for her again, then waited.

"Abby, I'm too tired for this nonsense. Come home, girl."

Nothing in return, only the silence of the April night sky around me and stirrings from the pasture. I walked back in, this time remembering to lock the door. I reassured myself Abby could sleep on the porch if that's what she preferred.

I stood for a minute and looked at August's rifle still propped up in the corner near the front door, its same resting place since the day after his funeral.

I wish you were here to help me, August. You'd know just what to do for this girl. You'd look directly at me, those deep eyes of yours and say, "It's your responsibility to save this girl's life, Hannah. Nothing is more important than that, not the border patrol, the current law they're arguing in Austin and DC, the gossip of the neighbors. Human life, that's where the buck stops."

I cried, standing in the hallway with the rifle in sight, only turning once toward the living room, where the girl slept. Everything in front of me seemed beyond my physical and emotional strength. Those bitter tears fell; I'd have to live this life without him and take care of this girl, alone. Because in this life, old widow women and little girls were vulnerable. Neither had the physical strength to fight the monsters as they travelled through fields, byways, and cities, running as fast as they could to catch their prey. It was a hateful world; I'd always known that, and I was raised never to expect anything to be fair. Nothing in life was a given. The only things I could control were my actions, including what happened in this house and on the land.

I thought of calling Buddy for help. My brother had always been good at keeping secrets. We'd been looking out for each other as long as I could remember, but Buddy was an old man, now. He was probably snoring in his recliner with the TV roaring full blast in front of him. I had no idea what I was facing with this poor girl asleep in my living room, but I wasn't going to drag a man in his eighties into this mess. If I even mentioned it to him, he'd fly down the dark road with a loaded rifle, never thinking if it was safe or not. He'd come because I asked him, but I couldn't do that to him. I loved him too much.

Then I thought of Joseph. His Spanish was a lot better than mine, and he was younger, stronger than any man I knew, including my own son. I looked at the clock on the kitchen wall. It was a little past ten. I was sure he was still up. I picked up my cell phone and called. His wife wouldn't appreciate it, but I had stopped worrying about Elizabeth's ever-changing moods a long time ago. Joseph answered on the third ring.

"Joseph, I need your help. If I thought it could wait until morning, I wouldn't have called this late."

I could hear Elizabeth in the background, "Who the hell is calling at this hour?"

"Did you hurt yourself, Hannah?"

"No, not at all. I found a girl coming back from the tornado anniversary Mass, maybe an hour or so after I saw you at church. She was in a ditch, semiconscious. She's probably been on the road for a while just by looking at her clothes, torn, very dirty. She's got some cuts and bruises, but no active bleeding. I brought her to the house. She might be a Mexican national, I don't know. She's not really responding to what little Spanish I can muster, but she's also exhausted. Joseph, your Spanish is better than mine. I need you here when she wakes up."

"Did you call the local or county sheriff? The county handles Texas runaways."

"I don't know if she's running from home or was brought across the border by a coyote. She could be involved in a trafficking ordeal. I suspect it's the latter. Now, I need to rest a few hours, but I'm setting the alarm for four. Can you be here around four thirty? Hoping she'll stay asleep until you get here."

"Hannah, did you call border patrol? The field office is right outside of town."

"No, Joseph, I'm calling you. Are you going to help me or not?"

"I'll be there at four thirty."

"Thank you. I'm sorry I even had to ask, but I couldn't think of anyone else to help me."

Before I could hang up, I heard Elizabeth's smart mouth.

"What does the queen want now? Doesn't matter. You'll run to her like you always have."

I waited for him to answer her, but he didn't.

"I'm sorry," was all I said before hanging up the phone. I imagined Joseph didn't answer Elizabeth's question. He probably just rolled over to his side of the bed until sleep came, same way he has handled her for the last forty years. My god, what a marriage.

CHAPTER SEVENTEEN

Hannah
Durand Ranch

I checked on her one more time before I set the alarm for a few hours of sleep. Sitting on the edge of the couch, I pulled the afghan around her neck, stroking her hair, loving her as if she were my own, the daughter August and I longed for all those years ago. Her breathing was steadier than earlier, her skin smooth beneath my touch. I whispered a few prayers, not knowing what the morning would bring. Maybe Joseph would have a better plan. My only plan was to not let her out of my sight, until I could find her family and get her home.

I pushed myself off the edge of the couch with my left arm; my right was shot, trembling from overuse. Standing above her, I sighed heavily, then pushed the curtains aside behind the couch. I couldn't see anything in the darkness. What stars were there earlier were hidden by low clouds, yet I searched for Abby, wondering why she didn't come when I called her. I pulled the curtains closed, creating a barrier between the monster in the dark and the girl.

I went to bed wearing the same clothes I wore to the tornado Mass. This was the second time in my life I had done that; once, when we buried August, and again tonight. I hoped this wasn't becoming a habit, but nothing had been right since he died. Nothing.

Kicking my shoes off, I fell into a deep sleep as soon as my head touched the pillow. I must have been asleep about an hour, the lamp still lit on the nightstand next to me, as I focused between its light and the need for more sleep. At first, I thought I was dreaming because I heard the sound of a locked door being forced open, although the sound was muffled, as if it came from a cave or an enclosed area, where I was a safe distance from any harm. But the sound of cracked wood, its splintering sending pieces of the front door falling like shards of glass across the threshold, jolted my senses. I strained to hear footsteps, willing my body to be alert despite the ache in every joint and the desperate need of sleep.

"This isn't a dream," every nerve within my spine screamed as adrenaline shot through my body like liquid nitrate. A powerful mixture of fear and instinct coursed through my body, shouting, "Someone is out there, someone is pushing the front door open, jimmied it with a tire iron. Get up. He has come to kill you and the girl!"

I knew then Abby was dead. The instinct I didn't trust earlier in the night, that the girl and I were being watched on the road, in the pasture, came back to me. Whoever was watching us killed my dog to silence her. I became physically ill with the regret of not heeding that warning as I put my shoes back on and looked at the alarm clock. It was 3:40 in the morning. All I needed to do was survive the next forty-five minutes until Joseph got here. But I knew, the minute I thought it, it was too late to wait for Joseph. It was up to me to defend myself and the girl. Me, a seventy-three-year-old woman.

I walked toward the front door, steadily, visualizing the feel of August's rifle in my hand, placing the butt of it against my shoulder, removing the safety latch, and aiming it at another human being. Killing someone didn't frighten me. I grew up around guns, even went deer hunting with my dad and brothers, happy to fill the freezer with venison for the family. I knew the full intent of pulling a trigger. Not once had I ever confused the finality of hunting or being hunted.

I walked past the living room. She was still sleeping with her knees pushed into her chest, subconsciously protecting her body from being touched. I kept walking, and the sound intensified, the frantic scrapping of the wooden door, the jolt of metal forced against it, wedging itself into the smallest of cracks, until it opened each time, a little more, a little more, a little more.

August's rifle was there next to the door. I picked it up and steadied the sight at the door handle. Unwavering, I waited for the monster on the other side to push his way through. I watched the file splinter the wood of the threshold, then the door, making the gap larger, until the monster pushed with all his might, and the door flung open. Unforgiving, I stared into his black eyes and pulled the trigger.

He fell backwards onto the threshold; the gaping wound in his forehead poured blood with his torso contorting, eyes bulging, pleading for life. I shot him again at close range, and a blur of red crossed before my eyes. Blood sprayed against me, the wall, the floor, and the door.

I don't know how much time went by from when I stood over the monster, pointing August's rifle at him, pulling the trigger again, watching the brilliant flash of red seep across my peripheral. It could have been five minutes. It could have been an hour. Time didn't matter. When I did look up, I saw Joseph in his truck, parked to the right of the porch. His eyes met mine in disbelief. Behind me, the girl was crouched near the sofa, spattered with flecks of blood and screaming.

I killed the monster.

CHAPTER EIGHTEEN

Ronnie Hoffman, Sheriff of Edwards County
Rocksprings, Texas

I got the call from Joseph around five that morning. It shocked me, to say the least. I'd known him all my life; he was just a few years ahead of me in high school, but that didn't mean we saw each other every day, much less talked to each other. I also knew his wife and daughters. Like everybody in this town, I've seen them at their best and worst. That was part of the job. Joseph was no different.

When his dad died and left his mom with a bunch of kids, all boys who went to work as soon as they could, it was Joseph and she who started making tamales for extra money. He didn't like it, but he did it, slipping and sliding in the grease of that little kitchen of theirs. Everybody in town bought the tamales made by Mrs. Gonzales. You had to get on a waiting list at Christmas time.

Joseph didn't like being part of the tamale business. When you went over to get your three or four dozen tamales for the Christmas season, he wouldn't look you in the face when he handed over the aluminum foil packages. But his mama did, blessing you, kissing your forehead, offering you a dulce de leche candy made with the pecans Joseph picked from the side of the road because they were free for the taking. She was a good woman, Mrs. Gonzales. Like most good women in this county, she worked herself into an early grave.

Joseph had a chip on his shoulder. What Mexican boy who grew up poor, without a daddy, didn't have a chip on his shoulder? That was life in a small Texas town. Rocksprings was no different with its prejudices. Hell, I grew up speaking English and Spanish, but I understood without being told, I was white, and there was a difference.

Joseph was a hard worker, just like his mama. There wasn't a man in this town who worked as hard as he did with search and rescue after the tornado of 1993. He never cried, not even when we pulled the Sheetrock and roof joist off a young mother and her toddler beneath her. That mother's arms were still spread across her daughter's body; even in death she protected her baby girl. He picked up those bodies, cradled each of them in his arms, and carried them to a temporary shelter we set up. Man, I cried, I cried the hardest when I watched that man cover those bodies with a sheet, make the sign of the cross over them, then return to pick up more bodies. He never stopped to rest, not even to eat or get a drink of water. So, yeah, the sound of his voice this morning, full of emotion, stumbling over words, stopped me dead in my tracks.

"You got to get out here, Ronnie. We got a dead man. Durand Ranch."

"Why are you out there at this hour? Damn, Joseph, your voice is shaking."

"Hannah called me. I'll explain when you get here. There's a possible runaway, maybe kidnap victim. Not sure. Better call an ambulance for the body."

"This is a helluva call to get this early in the morning. Is it secure?"

"No need for backup. Don't bring a bunch of fools with you to complicate things. We'll sort it out."

That was all he said before hanging up. I poured another cup of coffee for the ride, noting the sunrise was a brilliant orange, one of the prettiest I've seen in a long time.

It was close to an hour's drive to get to the Durand place, with a couple of cattle guard crossings and gravel roads slowing me down along the way. Once I crossed the last cattle guard, I saw a late model, four-door sedan parked to the right of the crossing. I got out and walked around it, noticing a pile of cigarette butts on the ground next to the front left tire. I called the plate numbers into dispatch.

I walked another half mile, looking for clues, and that's when I saw the family dog. She'd been stabbed in the face and neck, repeatedly. The grass was still wet with her blood and tissue.

When I finally pulled up to the porch, next to Joseph's truck, the first thing I noticed was his truck door was still open. The next thing I saw was the body of a Mexican man, covered in blood, right across the threshold of the broken front door. The entire area was covered in blood. It was hard to keep from sliding in it, as I held on to the broken frame of the door for added support.

Once I got closer to the body, it appeared the first shot was to the forehead, done with a rifle, left quite a hole. But the second shot, at close range, made the real mess. My immediate thought was a burglary, with this dead man casing the place for days, knowing Hannah lived out here alone. But why would Hannah call Joseph to help her? I knew he worked alongside them for years, but once August got older, he sold a lot of his animals. I wouldn't think there'd be much work for Joseph out here, especially in the last few years. But maybe Hannah kept him on, since August died, for general maintenance around the place.

I was confused by Joseph's mentioning of a runaway, maybe even a kidnap victim, sitting in the house with them. The whole setup was strange, even for Edwards County, a stone's throw from the violence on the border.

I walked straight through the threshold and found Hannah, Joseph, and a young Mexican girl sitting in the living room. The girl sat close to Hannah, a blanket across her, even in this early morning heat. Hannah and Joseph met my eyes, without saying a word. All three of them looked like death warmed over. I supposed it had been a hell of a night.

I sat down next to Joseph and took out a notepad and pen. Despite the fact I've known Hannah and Joseph my entire life, I couldn't make them think they'd be given special privileges because of that. Hell, it was my job. The more I stuck to being the man in charge, the better off we'd all be.

"Hannah, I'm going to ask some questions. I've already called an ambulance for the corpse. Can you tell me what you know about the dead man?"

She looked at me, then down at the notebook in my hand, as if it were a living thing, a breathing recorder of last night's event and her interpretation of it. Then steadily, as if completely aware of every breath she took, every word she spoke, she explained to me what happened.

"I killed him. Shot him twice. He was breaking into my home. I don't know if he was after the girl or both of us. I picked her up, last night, maybe an hour or so after the tornado Mass at the church. I haven't been able to communicate much with her because of my poor Spanish, so I don't know if she's a kidnap victim or a runaway. She's in bad shape, physically and mentally. I called Joseph before all of this happened, hoping he could speak to her, find the help she needed. His Spanish is far better than mine. He agreed to come out early, but before he got here, the man I killed tried to break into the house. I know this is Texas, Sheriff, where the Nineteenth Amendment is considered the root of all evil, but surely you're not going to haul a seventy-three-year-old woman in for questioning. I was protecting my property."

I ignored her sarcasm, just like I did the concern on Joseph's face.

"Looks like you used a rifle, Hannah. Where is it?"

"It's August's rifle. I put it in the shed, because it was a mess. I've got a big enough mess with the front door and the porch. I tried to keep it as far away from her eyes, hoping it would help her calm down." Hannah looked over at the girl next to her, smiling sadly. "Anyway, the rifle was next to the front door, before all this happened. Sam put it there the day after August's funeral. I guess he thought it would make me feel a bit more secure being out here alone, without his father."

I smiled at her, nodding my head. Then I put my foot in my mouth.

"I'm going to call border patrol about the girl. I'll take her and the rifle when I leave."

"No, you won't."

The girl looked up at Hannah. She probably recognized the words border patrol. Hannah placed a protective arm around the girl's shoulders.

"Now, Hannah, I'm going to remind you of this very specific law. When someone enters the US without following immigration laws, it's a crime. Those who help people with illegal entry, or those who assist people after an illegal entry, can be charged with the crime of harboring an undocumented immigrant. You know this. Besides, this girl could be a drug mule."

"You don't even know her story, Sheriff, and you've made up your mind. None of us know her story, and we aren't going to jump to conclusions like some renegade mob, because of the color of her skin, and the fact she doesn't speak English. We're going to treat her like a human being, period. She hasn't had a bath, eaten a decent meal in God knows when. Plus, Joseph hasn't had a chance to talk to her. It all happened so fast, we're still in shock, especially her. Just take that body on the porch with you. You can come out later with the border patrol and resume your talk about laws and living near the border."

"Hannah, I am the law. There's no need to fight me. I can see this was a forced entry just by looking at the front door. You need to calm down."

"You're right, Sheriff. I'll calm down. I'm fixing a pot of coffee and some breakfast. That's my job right now. I expect you to do yours."

She left the room, taking the girl with her. I heard a back bedroom door close, then Hannah reappeared in the kitchen, rinsing a coffeepot out at the sink.

"Joseph, the conversation isn't over. I know y'all are half crazy right now with what just happened, but I need some help. Can you get something to secure the front entrance of the house? That ambulance will be here any minute. I'll need to take some pictures of the crime scene."

"Let me explain again, Sheriff. No crime was committed here. I was protecting my home and two lives," Hannah said from the kitchen.

Joseph nodded at me. I stood, looked out the bay window, and saw the ambulance approaching the house. I didn't want to tell her. God knows I waited as long as I could, but I had to. I walked into the kitchen and took the coffee mug she offered me.

"Hannah, I found your dog when I drove up. Looks like the man you shot killed her, probably to keep her quiet last night. Tell me what I can do for her. I'll bury her out on the land, maybe where I found her. If you'd like that."

Those green eyes flashed back at me. She was a hell of a woman.

"I knew Abby was dead. She never came when I called her. Sheriff, take Joseph, and show him where Abby is. I want her back here, near the oak tree by the front porch. August and I spent many nights with her on that porch, talking to each other, playing the accordion. Sometimes we didn't talk at all, just enjoyed the peace and quiet. That's a good resting place for Abby, that tree."

"Yes, ma'am."

CHAPTER NINETEEN

Hannah
Durand Ranch

"You're harboring an illegal and killed a man?"

I looked out the living room window, watching the sheriff take photos of the man I killed. Minutes later the EMT men put him on a gurney and drove off. Sheriff Hoffman followed the ambulance in his pickup truck. My son's voice on the telephone seemed hundreds of miles away from the scene before me, even a century away, compared to the new reality out the living room window.

"Mom, are you there? Talk to me. Who's over at the house now?"

"I'm here, Sam. Just tired. Joseph and the girl are here with me at the house. Sheriff Hoffman left. I'm sure he'll be back with the border patrol."

"Did you call a lawyer, Mom?"

"No, why should I? I was protecting my property and two lives. I've done nothing wrong."

"I'll get a lawyer for you, then I'm on my way."

"Sammy, let's talk about this first, before you bring another person in on it. The more people involved, the more complicated it becomes, and the longer it will take to get this poor girl home to her family. When you come, stay a few days. I hope that won't be a problem for your family."

"I'll be there in an hour or two after I talk to Leslie and let work know. But I'm telling you now for your own good, you've got to have a lawyer. Let the authorities take care of this girl. She's not your responsibility."

"She is my responsibility. I found her, thank God, and now, she's a guest in my home. A guest, Sam. The same way I'd treat every human being out there in need. You were taught this as a child. You need to also remember I've walked this earth a lot longer than you have, and I've been okay so far in the decisions I've made."

"Mom, you're seventy-three years old. Face it. This is way out of your control now. A man is dead, and an illegal is living in the house. Laws were broken, and you may be implicated. I'm not a lawyer, but I'm getting one. I'm begging you not to do anything else until I get there."

"Yes, Sam. I'm seventy-three, still breathing, and the heart is still beating. I'm just as much aware of what I'm doing as you are."

I hung up the phone before he could get another word in and returned to the living room, where Joseph and the girl were talking. I sat next to her.

"Hannah, her name is Ariela Morales."

I put my arms around her, looked directly into her eyes, and said, "Ariela."

"She's from Zaragoza, Mexico. Was kidnapped about a week ago with her friend, Katia Hernández. The man you shot killed the other girl in one of those cheap motels hunters stay in during deer season. Ariela ran from there; you picked her up afterwards."

I looked at Ariela. Her eyes were closed against Joseph's words. Although a different language, the sound of her murdered friend's name spoken out loud caused her to shrink right before my eyes. That pain would take a long time to heal.

"How far is Zaragoza from here?"

He reached for his phone in his back pocket.

"A little over three hours."

"Let's take her home, Joseph. Now."

"What? We can't do that. The sheriff is coming back with state and federal people."

"Exactly. They might want to put her in a detention center until all the facts surface. She didn't ask to come here. She's not a criminal."

"You know how dangerous it is without us even talking about it. The cartel or a gang might still be looking for her. She's a payday for men like that. They'll want their investment back."

Hannah gave him a steady look

Joseph sighed. "Okay, I know I won't change your mind. After forty years working on this ranch, I've never known you to quit on anything.

You're stubborn, Hannah. I'll help you, but we need to be smart about this, particularly with Hoffman. The sooner we get out of here, the better. We got to leave before he gets back."

"Give me a little over an hour. I'll meet you in town, but I want to talk to Father Flores before we go. I'll bring Ariela with me, go by the bank, and fill the truck up. Meet us at the church. You can park the truck in the back by the rectory if you're worried about people seeing it."

"I'll need to tell my wife, Hannah."

"We'll come back tonight, Joseph. Don't tell her where we're going. It will be all over town in an hour if you do."

"I still need to tell her I'm leaving, but I won't tell her where I'm going."

"Of course, you need to tell her. She's your wife, though she's made you miserable for years. Forgive me for saying that, but it's true."

I had too much to do to wait for a reply from him, so I left him standing there with his heart in his hand, expecting me to say something else. There was nothing else to say. I needed to take Ariela home, and I needed him to help me.

"Ariela, *te llevaré a casa. Su casa.*"

She smiled at me, understanding every word of my Spanish. It was the first time I saw light in her eyes since I found her. What fears and doubts I had were eased by that smile. In a short time, I had come to love her, yes, love her like a daughter. Many people think a woman's mothering instinct leaves when her last child leaves home. It doesn't. It pangs at the heart, the longing to hold a baby again. The urge to be needed as a woman doesn't die once you're menopausal. It only intensifies. I've learned things in all these years, things I'd give to her, freely. I'd never be lonely out here with her. We could share this house and ranch. She could go to school here, and I would give her everything I could to help her succeed. There was one fact preventing all these dreams from coming true: she wasn't my daughter.

I had a son and grandchildren. Thinking of Sammy, I realized how soon I had to get out of here before he showed up. It would hurt him when he realized I lied. But I also knew he wouldn't let me take Ariela home. His heart was not as generous as mine nor his father's; besides, he hadn't lived the life Ariela had. Why would he be generous with a stranger, who hadn't had the advantages he had? He'd be in league with the sheriff and border patrol, because it was the law, by the book. I couldn't fight all of them, so it was best to leave now.

I took Ariela's hand and we walked to the bedroom, searching for a pair of jeans and a tee shirt that might fit her. The clothes she was wearing when she came here didn't wash well, despite all the bleach and hot water I used. I couldn't get those stains out. In Sam's old bedroom, I kept a drawer full of clothes my grandsons left over the years. No matter how many times I reminded them and Leslie, they never took those clothes home with them.

I found an old pair of Will's jeans, a tee shirt, and a sweatshirt. They were a good fit for her. My tennis shoes were a bit too big, but she wore them with a pair of August's socks, so the heel didn't move with every step she took.

With both of us wearing ball caps to protect our faces from the West Texas sun, we went to the kitchen, where we made peanut butter and jelly sandwiches. Once she was comfortable with finishing the job herself, I wrote a note to Sam.

Dear Son,
Please don't worry about me. I'm sorry I even called you this
morning and got you involved. I'll explain when I get back tonight.
Stay here and wait for me. I'm sure the sheriff and border patrol will
be back out here, so when you're done with this note, get rid of it.
Trust me as I have always trusted you to do the right thing.

I love you, Sam.
Mama

Before we left the ranch, I called Buddy on my cell. He didn't pick up after the fourth ring, probably in town with his oldest daughter, Karla, picking up a few groceries. I decided not to leave a message. Things were already too complicated, and I was growing tired by the minute.

We left thirty minutes later. Ariela sat next to me on the bench seat of the truck. I only looked back once before crossing the last cattle guard on the ranch, remembering the nights August and I sat on the porch with Abby at our feet. The accordion strapped to my chest, fingers flying across the keys, and the sound of a German waltz mingling with the wind were reminders of the beautiful life we lived. But now, the farther I drove away from the ranch and memories, the more I accepted today's reality. That peaceful life I lived was gone forever because a monster stole two little girls, then raped and murdered Katia. I felt no remorse for killing him, just as I thought nothing about breaking a law to get her home. My flesh and blood compasses, Grandma Schoen and Uncle Rudy, wouldn't have hesitated to save Ariela Morales's life, no matter what the cost.

CHAPTER TWENTY

Hannah

Rocksprings, Texas

Father Flores was in his office when I walked in with Ariela. He came to St. Mary's in Rocksprings just two years ago and was loved by almost everyone. There were some naysayers who didn't trust him because he was a Jesuit.

Many, including me, thought him to be a great communicator, uniting the Hispanic and Anglo parishioners with his bilingual homilies and quiet approach to problems within the community. A true Jesuit, he established a preschool for the children of working parents and GED classes for adults and teen dropouts. Classes were taught by retired teachers, giving them a chance to share their love for learning, as well as making them feel needed again. With the tiny donations Father received, he refurbished an old meeting room in the church and purchased desks, books, a chalkboard, and five new computers. The room was named in honor of another Jesuit, Pope Frances.

Like Pope Frances, Father Flores believed in social justice. His homilies were often tinged with passion for job development and better housing in the community. Some people loved him for it; others simply couldn't stand him, accused him of showing off like a politician and not giving a decent homily according to Church tradition. It was the same sad fact about human nature, and how others treated any man or woman who wanted to bring change to an institution. The gossip about Father Flores was horrific. He was always in a damned if I do, damned if I don't situation with the parishioners.

I saw Father Flores as a man who loved God's people, regardless of their past mistakes, including those parishioners who had divorced or weren't faithful to Church tradition. But tradition is a line drawn in the sand for many, especially since the Church has existed since the first century AD. Risk takers and visionaries often suffered when tradition was challenged. Father Flores was no exception.

A native of Nuevo Laredo, he spent his youth between the two cultures of the US and Mexico, although he was never accepted as a native of either culture. Such was the life of a man without a country and few friends, because he chose to wear a white band around his neck.

I was his friend. August was too, until the day he died. We respected him for his work, but most of all, we loved him because he loved the people in the church. I couldn't leave for Mexico with Ariela and Joseph without having his blessing, although I noticed Ariela began biting her nails the minute we arrived at the church. I took her right hand gently from her mouth and held it in mine for a few seconds, looking into her eyes and repeated over and over, "It will be okay, Ariela. *El Padre Flores es un buen hombre.*"

After he welcomed us into his office, he motioned for us to sit in the two chairs in front of his desk, then looked carefully at Ariela before speaking to me. When my eyes met his, I knew he understood she was a victim of a terrible crime.

"Father, I'm taking this young lady home to Zaragoza, Mexico. She was kidnapped by a trafficker who broke into the house. I shot and killed him." I realized after saying it, how insane it all sounded, like a B-grade script for a movie filmed along the border. My spoken words were as erratic as the timeline and my pounding heart. When I had a second to breathe after speaking, I felt my blood pressure rising again. I was so tired of repeating what happened over and over again, but I couldn't give in to it. Not now.

He looked at me without speaking, waiting for me to continue.

"The sheriff has been to the house. I'm leaving in just a few minutes with Joseph Gonzales. We'll drive her home, together, before the border patrol gets involved."

"Yes, Hannah, continue . . . " He pushed his hair across his forehead, then smiled patiently at both of us.

"I am asking for a blessing, Father. For me and . . . " I hesitated, then drew Ariela closer to me. She was shaking.

"Ariela Morales," I said, trying not to cry. I hated myself for being weak and old, but the job before me seemed more than this old woman could muster.

Father made the sign of the cross, then placed his hands on both of our bowed heads, and said a prayer. He then reclined in his desk chair and looked at me and Ariela.

"I can see you are determined to do this, Hannah. I won't stop you. It's a brave thing but very dangerous on many levels. Joseph will be a tremendous help to you with the language and navigation."

"Father, if I don't return, I want you to talk to my son. Tell him about this meeting. Tell him I felt it my responsibility as a human being to help this girl."

"Yes."

"Please let my brother, Buddy, know as well. I'd rather him hear it from you than anyone else. You may not remember him, Father. He doesn't always attend Mass regularly, but he thinks the world of you."

He stood up from his chair and hugged me, then gently touched Ariela's shoulder, speaking directly to her.

"*No tengas miedo, niña. Esta noche estarás en casa con tu madre y tu padre.*"

She smiled at him when he told her she'd be with her family tonight. I put her hand in mine, and we left the church. The beginning of the hot spring winds pushed the dust from the church's parking lot back into the opened windows of the truck. Ariela coughed. I patted her leg for reassurance, as I drove toward the First Bank of Rocksprings, thinking a thousand or so in cash would be enough for the trip. There'd be no need for me to leave her alone in the truck while I went in. It was an easy withdraw from the window. The tellers knew me. Like any small-town business, the women at the bank had been working here forever, and I'd been their customer forever.

As we waited behind Jan Walker's late-model Mustang, noticing the colored smoke and smell of leaking oil from its exhaust, I thought of Joseph. I knew Elizabeth would give him trouble. She was a bitter woman, spewing her poison to anyone within earshot. Her daughters were no different. Even when they were little girls, I'd see them lined up next to their mother on a church pew, scowls on their faces. Elizabeth's biggest problem was the one she created all by herself—she never realized Joseph was a good man; she expected more than he could give and was ungrateful for what she had. But I've come to realize most women don't appreciate their husbands.

CHAPTER TWENTY-ONE

Leslie

Alamo Heights, San Antonio

Crazy Connie as a mother was finally upstaged by my mother-in-law. I didn't think it possible in a million years, but with her out on the land by herself for months, thinking she could run the place by herself, I knew something bad was going to happen. Easter was a disaster with the boys, too emotional, Sam shouting at the kids. Aaron couldn't wait to get out of there, and I'm sure that will be his last visit for a long time.

Now, I knew she was having a bad time. Her appearance wasn't the same, although Hannah was never one to wear makeup or do something with her hair outside of a braid or ponytail. She didn't even color it. But her whole demeanor at Easter was that of a sad, old woman. We should have brought her to San Antonio then and put a for sale sign on that ranch. Nobody needed the continued stress of managing it, but now, we had a real mess on our hands. Sam was beside himself this morning, pacing the kitchen and drinking cup after cup of coffee.

"I've got to get her an attorney, Leslie. Help me with some contacts, make some phone calls, I guess a criminal lawyer, hell, I don't know."

"You're going to have a heart attack if you don't sit down, right now, and take a breath. I can see the blood vessels bulging in your neck from here. And for God's sake, don't drink any more coffee."

"I told her I was on my way. Let me call the office and get a shower."

"I'll pack an overnight bag for you while you shower, but sit down, Sam. Come on. You've got time to hear this. Please convince your mom to sell the land. It's too much for her out there all alone; now, we got this mess to deal with, and it's going to be as hard for you as it is for her. Honey, the

96

boys don't even want to go out there anymore; the days of them spending a summer with their grandparents out on the land are over. Your dad is gone. Your mom is in trouble. Now, I'm sure it was breaking and entering, self-defense. I don't know what to think about this illegal she's got with her. Maybe that dead man was a coyote.

"We need an attorney. I'll call Greg Abrams." Sam knew I played tennis with Greg's wife. "I'll phone him once you're on the road. Now, get your shower, baby. We'll figure this out together."

My mother was the queen of extroverts. Crazy Connie didn't know a stranger. Of course, every stranger knew her. But Hannah—she was an introvert. So was August. They were very private people. To think of her taking an illegal into her house, a total stranger, well, it floored me. It made me wonder what she had been doing out on the ranch by herself since August died.

I didn't care if a cent never went to me from the sale of the land. I didn't. But if my boys could benefit, if it could truly change their life in the type of education they received, I don't know why their grandmother and father wouldn't support it. Once Sam was back tomorrow, we'd look into some retirement homes in the area. It would help keep his mind off Hannah's problems for a few hours. We should probably treat ourselves to a nice lunch in town, along the River Walk, maybe even drink a few margaritas together. Now that was something we hadn't done together in years. Once Sam was relaxed, I'd mention the need for a realtor for the ranch. I could handle finding one, just like getting Hannah a lawyer.

The only sticky thing about talking to Greg Abrams about representing Hannah was how to begin the story. "Hey Greg, it's Leslie, your wife and I play tennis together. Do you have time to take my mother-in-law's case in Rocksprings? At seventy-three years old, she's shot a man dead and has an illegal minor living with her."

It was shocking even by Texas standards. But I was Crazy Connie's daughter. I got over being shocked and embarrassed by the time I was twelve. I'd see this one through, too.

CHAPTER TWENTY-TWO

Joseph
Rocksprings, Texas

I wasn't surprised to find her still in bed when I got home from Hannah's. She must have gotten up and watched TV after I left. The coffee table held the paper plate she ate from, next to her dead cell phone. But that wasn't unusual for her. It was her lifestyle since the girls moved out. Sometimes it killed me, thinking of the girl, the young wife she used to be. Pretty Elizabeth, her body against mine, willingly. Elizabeth cooking for the family. Elizabeth loving me without resentment. I was just as much to blame for the life we lived now.

I just never loved her, not really. I've tried to find the reasons why. Maybe I worked too much, kept to myself too much, but I didn't need the constant approval she did. In the beginning of our marriage, I thought it was part of discovering each other, as a husband and wife, exploring our sensuality together, without Elizabeth feeling any shame about having sex outside of marriage like she did when I got her pregnant. She was much more relaxed in the bedroom as my wife.

I was happy for both of us, and complimented her as much as I could when she wore a sexy nightgown or tried a new hair style. She needed me to look at her. She needed to hear I wanted her, but I didn't always say the things she wanted to hear. I didn't grow up in a house where a man constantly reminded a woman how desirable she was. My father was dead. Mama worked like a dog, cooking, cleaning for every penny she made. Maybe I just never learned to love Elizabeth.

Besides, by the time I got home from work and ate, I was tired. I stayed in the ranching business my entire life, despite the years that kept slowing me down, feeling every sack of feed I lifted in my knees and back. In my joints, I felt every blue norther that froze the land while I worked outdoors, moving animals into barns or digging fence posts to keep them in pastures. Elizabeth knew my job, its physical demands on my body, but it didn't change her dependence on me.

I guess she tried it all, the shoes, the clothes, the nails, manicured and blood red. I wasn't blind to any of it. I appreciated it, but I didn't tell her. I just assumed she knew. Hell, I brought home a good paycheck, took a hundred-dollar bill out for myself, and gave her the rest. I never questioned how she handled the money. And that was from the very beginning of our marriage. I had my job, and hers was to manage the home and our family. She did pretty much what she wanted to do during the day, but over time, that didn't matter. She went from trying to please me to demanding I pay attention to her. Her humiliation and anger only drove me further away, because I couldn't deal with being the man who let her down. The man who didn't love his wife.

Once our girls were old enough to be less work for her, she stopped trying. She might have been tired, tired of me and this town. She withdrew into herself, and I got exactly what I deserved, silence and space. Lots of space, even though we shared the same bed. I couldn't breathe in that bed without smelling or touching her; but intimacy, it was gone a long time ago.

It seemed like all of it came down to this morning and finding her still in bed, sleeping. I didn't bother being quiet when I began packing a small duffle bag. I wanted the noise to wake her, make her mad. The last thing I could stomach was touching her shoulder or calling her name, any kind of tenderness like that might give her the illusion I cared. A better man might have been kinder. I just wanted to be an honest man, not a man silenced by responsibility like I had been.

I turned on the closet light and stood in front of the row of long-sleeve shirts I had. When I thought how many shirts I needed for this trip, I realized I didn't know when I'd be coming back from Zaragoza, even though Hannah thought it would be tonight. I knew better. Nothing in Mexico was solved in a day. I took two shirts off their hangers and put them in the duffle bag.

"Turn the damn light off," she said, rolling over to face me.

"Elizabeth, I'm leaving."

"You're leaving. Where to?"

She reached over to turn on the bedside lamp, then viewing the time on the alarm clock as 7:15 a.m., she turned the lamp off, readjusted the comforter, and pulled it up to her neck.

"It doesn't matter where I'm going. Don't know how long I'll be gone. I may not be coming back." When I said those words, I realized I might not return from Mexico alive. It might also be my last chance with Hannah. I turned off the closet light and closed the door.

"Are you divorcing me?" Her eyes were open, watching every move I made from the closet to the dresser, where I put socks, boxers, and a tee shirt into a duffle bag.

"You can tell everyone you're divorcing me, if it makes it easier." I was glad she said it first. Divorce. Now it was out there, never to be taken back.

This caused her to sit up in bed, and in the early morning light, I almost thought I was looking at Elizabeth, the sixteen-year-old girl I knew all those years ago. Her face was a confusion of hurt and anger, like so many teenage girls in love for the first time.

"Are you going somewhere with Hannah? Now that she's a widow, it's easier for both of you, isn't it? You get her and the land, Joseph. Something you've wanted since we were kids. I'm not a stupid woman."

She pulled the lamp on the nightstand out of the socket and threw it at me. It hit the wall near the dresser, leaving an imprint in the Sheetrock.

I picked it up and put it back on the dresser, avoiding her eyes, knowing full well it was a gutless thing to do.

"Elizabeth, things haven't been good between us for a while, and time is the one thing we don't have a whole lot of. Don't you want to find someone to love you the way I couldn't, before it's too late?"

"You selfish man. I've been sitting around for over forty years thinking that part of you would change. You'd stop sulking, look around and appreciate me and the family. But you didn't. You really think Hannah is in love with you? She's missing her dead husband. That's all. You're not going to get her and the ranch."

This time I looked at her.

"Shut up."

"You never loved me, Joseph. Never. You got me pregnant and married me. The right thing to do for the time we lived in and who we were. But

I've been naïve. A stupid woman, really, thinking if I loved you enough, you'd eventually love me back. What a hell of a life I've made for myself, basing it all on hope. It wore me out, and just look at what I got in return. Nothing. Nothing at all."

Her hurt was real, but it didn't stop me. I didn't even look back at her in the bed, sobbing uncontrollably. I kept moving forward, grabbing my toothbrush and deodorant out of the bathroom, then walking out the door and out of that marriage. None of it was planned. It just happened, and like so many things in my life, I responded to the initial shock by moving forward. The sound of the dead bolt mechanism clicked, telling me this part of my life was over.

I sat in the truck for a few minutes, going over the Texas map I had in the glove box. Driving to Mexico wasn't a big deal. I'd been doing that since I was a kid, although today's border was different from the one in the seventies, even the eighties—we crossed the Rio Grande then like crossing the street. A little over six hours driving, there and back to Rocksprings, maybe Hannah's place or a motel. I didn't know where I would land. I just kept moving toward the plans she made for Mexico. I couldn't figure out if I was being overconfident by following Hannah blindly, but it didn't matter. I'd given her my word. And for the first time in a long time I felt good about something.

I folded the map and placed it on top of my Colt Gov. model 1911, slamming the glove box closed. Thinking about the .45 in there was a reminder of who I was as a boy and a man. That gun was the only thing I inherited from my father. The only thing that didn't come with an installment payment or regret. Backing out of the driveway this morning was one of the easiest things I've ever done in my life.

I drove to the church like a teenage boy, windows down, radio blaring, in my anticipation of seeing Hannah. Turning into the church parking lot, I drove toward the rectory. My mind wasn't on Zaragoza or the girl. I blocked the sight of the dead man shot at close range on Hannah's front porch like it was something I saw a lifetime ago. All I thought about was her. Maybe Elizabeth was right. Maybe I was a fool, just an old man thinking I still had a chance to be loved by a woman like Hannah.

CHAPTER TWENTY-THREE

Sheriff Hoffman

Durand Ranch

When I got back out to Hannah's place with Victor Cruz from border patrol following close behind, someone had walked right through the crime tape I put around the front. That someone was Sam. He was sitting at the kitchen table with his head in his hands. A handwritten letter was in front of him on the table. Agent Cruz was practically walking on my heels, so there was no way I could offer Sam any support besides business as usual.

"Where is she, Ronnie?" Sam asked, handing me the letter in his hand.

"I suspect she left with the girl she found, Ariela Morales. She seemed very protective of her, Sam. Almost maternal."

"Well, that's what the note says, but I didn't have time to throw it away. So, hell, what do we do now?"

Agent Cruz picked up the note from the table and began reading it, then placed it in a little ziplock bag he took out of his back pocket. I gave him the eye, letting him know from the get-go who was running the show here. My town, my county, my case. *Stay in your own lane, Cruz.* I knew most of the agents in town by first name, but the new guy in front of me was nothing like the other agents. Cruz was all about protocol. From the spotless government-issued truck he drove, proudly displaying U.S. Customs and Border Protection, to his starched field uniform. The other agents became friends; we understood each other, the area we lived in, and the people we protected. I'd never allow a rogue agent here, bullying my people, acting as a one-man vigilante determined to make the border spic-and-span. It wasn't going to happen this century or any other. People were messy, and the border was even worse. It always had been, always would be. Time would tell what Cruz was all about. Right now, he had used up ninety percent of the patience he'd get from me for the day.

I returned my focus on Sam, knowing he thought his mother was probably in Mexico or close to it. I suspected she was dead, along with the girl. The man Hannah killed had accomplices, and there'd be no way they'd let an old woman get away with killing one of their men. But I couldn't tell Sam that, not now. I had to piecemeal it to him because I didn't think he could stomach it. Sam was not the man his father was. He was the spoiled only child of a big ranch owner. He was doing pretty good being middle-aged and fighting San Antonio traffic, but he knew nothing about hard times, times like an old woman shooting a man to death and running off to Mexico with an illegal. I couldn't even make this one up, it was so damn crazy. But that was my line of work, not Sam's in his nice temperature-controlled office, pushing paper around. Maybe I'd just take my time feeding him information. I didn't need him butting into this case. Cruz was enough.

"For now, I need to tell you what happened here last night, Sam."

"I know what happened here. I talked to my mother on the phone, apparently before she changed her mind and wrote this note. A note, for God's sake, and goes off to Mexico after shooting a man dead. What the hell? The thought of her driving that girl back to Mexico makes me sick to my stomach. She's seventy-three years old. I should have never let her stay out here after Dad died. A lot of this is my fault."

I glanced over at Cruz. He was recording everything Sam said on one of those electronic tablets, making it increasingly difficult for me to wrap this case up without the Feds involved.

"Your mother had Joseph Gonzales over here after everything went down with the intruder. I'm sure he knows a lot more about her going to Mexico. I'll go by his place and talk to him. Meanwhile, just stay put. We don't need to let this get out of control, more than it already has," I said, looking directly at Cruz. He never looked up at me, just continued writing everything down in that fancy-ass tablet of his. I shouldn't have mentioned going by the Gonzales house. He probably thought he'd ride shotgun over there with me.

"Thank you, Ronnie. Do you know if she took Abby with her?"

"Abby's dead. Joseph buried her earlier this morning out by that oak, near the porch."

"Dead?"

"She was stabbed to death by the intruder."

"Jesus. Who the hell was this guy?"

"A monster, for sure. Just stay put. I'll call you when I know something."

I was almost in town when Deputy Stancik called, hysterical and talking way too fast. Of course, that wasn't unusual for him. He started his day every day with those giant cans of liquid energy. Within an hour, he was bouncing off the walls, knocking things over, and spitting all over himself when he talked.

"Sheriff, I got a call from the Big Buck Motel about thirty minutes ago. Maid found the body of a Mexican girl in one of the rooms. I'm at the motel now."

"Slow down, Tony, so I can understand you. Got your heart racing on caffeine. First question. Why didn't you call me when you first got the call?"

"Well, sir, I didn't think it was a big deal at the time. All kinds of transients driving up and down Highway 57, picking up working girls and bringing them back to the motel for party time. Remember that incident a few months ago with that nut from California in the minivan? He tore the motel room up, set the mattress on fire, then left the water running in the shower and sink just for spite."

"Get to the point, Tony."

"Well, yes sir, when I got here after the call, I walked on over to the room, located way in the back parking lot. The door was wide open. That poor Mexican girl had her throat slit, straight across. Mattress was soaked through to the carpet with her blood."

"Who was working when these people checked in?"

"I grilled the dipshit who runs the place. The clerk on shift that night said the man that registered was a Mexican, in his thirties, big man, long hair worn in a ponytail. Signed the registry as Pancho Villa. He paid in cash. He's the only one anyone ever saw. No one heard anything from the room, no arguing, nothing. I'm sure the manager was lying, sir. He never hears anything when it comes to all the stuff that happens in that place. That night clerk was probably scared to death, turned out all the lights, and hid under the furniture in that front office."

"Yep. Too bad the clerk wasn't smart enough to catch the name Pancho Villa. I'll meet you out there. Secure the area. No one in the room, not even the motel employees. Stand right in front of that closed door until I get there, deputy. I got one more stop. Won't take me long."

"Yes, sir."

I looked in the rearview mirror, and Agent Cruz was following closely. He was practically on my back bumper, making it tough for me to swing into Martha's for a quick breakfast burrito before I drove to Joseph's place. Now, the mess over at the motel pretty much sealed the deal on breakfast for me, but it also connected Ariela Morales's story. I looked at the opened package of white powdered donuts resting in the cupholder. Food is food when you're hungry. I ate the last three donuts and washed it down with the coffee Hannah gave me an hour ago, hoping I still remembered how to get out to Joseph's place.

Joseph and Elizabeth lived on a few acres about a mile east of town, in a small brick house they built in the eighties. I knew Elizabeth in high school, just like I knew Joseph. She used to be a pretty girl, but she put on a few pounds over the years. She didn't smile as much as she used to, either. I rarely saw the two of them together, but that wasn't so unusual for middle-aged couples, once the kids moved out. When years of marriage leave you looking for things to say to each other just to keep a conversation going, you start doing your own thing.

I parked close to the house with Cruz still on my tail. The first thing I noticed was Joseph's truck wasn't parked in the driveway, and someone had left the garage door open. Elizabeth's SUV was in there, though. Maybe Joseph was in a hurry this morning. I went ahead and walked around the side yard, turning around once to see if Cruz was following me. Of course, he was. Joseph's truck wasn't parked out by the back pasture, either.

I headed to the front door, but Cruz beat me to it with his tablet and a pencil behind his ear. *What the hell was the pencil for?* I bet his tablet ran out of juice, which was why I never wanted one. More trouble than they're worth. You never have to worry about plugging in a wooden pencil.

"Cruz, you've already knocked four times. Give her a chance to get to the door. It's still early."

Ignoring me, he kept knocking until Elizabeth swung the door open, wearing a house coat, with no shoes on her feet.

"Bit early don't you think, Sheriff? Who's your friend?

Before I could answer the woman, he spoke right up. "Agent Cruz with the border patrol."

"Shut up, Cruz," I said, reminding him I was still in charge of this investigation.

"Why is border patrol knocking on my door this morning, Ronnie?"

"I wanted to talk to Joseph. His truck isn't here, I see."

"You get an A for detective skills, Sheriff. Yep, and I don't know when he's coming back. I imagine he's with Hannah somewhere. He was over there about four this morning on a big secret mission. I bet he's still on that mission. Maybe they've eloped, but I guess you got to get a divorce before you can marry another woman."

"Liz, a lot of stuff happened out at that ranch early this morning. I can't explain it now, but if you talk to Joseph, you tell him to call me. I've tried his cell phone several times. He's not picking up."

"I'm not my husband's keeper. I guess that's fairly obvious to you, since he's with another woman. So, don't call me, text me, none of it. I don't want to be involved with the schemes of an old woman and a stupid man who has been following her around for decades with his tongue hanging out. As for your agent friend here, Joseph and I are US citizens, though you might have been fooled by the skin color."

She slammed the door closed.

CHAPTER TWENTY-FOUR

Ariela

Rocksprings, Texas and West Texas

No matter how hard I tried, paying close attention to the shapes her lips made, watching her eyes look into mine, I still couldn't understand much of what she said to me. I wanted to please the señora, so I smiled at her and listened with everything in me, concentrating on every syllable she said, often Spanish and English words mixed together, making my neck muscles knot and my head pound. After a while, I gave up and lied to her with a big smile on my face, nodding my head and saying, "*Sí, lo entiendo*, Señora Hannah." Inside my heart I cried, wishing I could understand her.

But everything the priest said to me I understood, especially when he told me, "*Esta noche estarás en casa con tu madre y tu padre.*" I prayed Father was right and I'd be with my family tonight in our little home in Zaragoza. Those were the most beautiful words a priest has ever said to me. And I believed Father Flores, yes, all of them, Señora Hannah and her friend, Joseph. Joseph's Spanish was as good as the priest's. They were my friends and wanted to help me. I believed this with all my heart, but the two men in the uniforms, I didn't trust. I knew what they wanted to do; they wanted to give me to some other federales, so they wouldn't have to deal with me anymore. A detention center in a desert is where they wanted to put me, locked in a cage like an animal; then I'd be someone else's problem, passed on and on, mi familia never knowing where I was, whether I was dead or alive. But Señora Hannah wouldn't let them. Maybe she was the woman's voice I heard last night. Maybe Santa Madre sent her to me, a white abuela with long grey hair and kind green eyes. Santa Maria gave me a guardian angel.

The señora and I sat inside her truck parked behind the priest's little house, waiting for Joseph to come. I already ate one of the sandwiches I made, not because I was hungry, but because I was nervous. The longer we stayed in Texas, the longer it would take to get to Mexico. Maybe there were more bad men out on the road. I was afraid of them finding me, but the señora wasn't. She smiled at me, offering a bottle of water after I finished my sandwich.

I heard a truck moving across the gravel parking lot behind the church. The señora looked up from her cell phone. Together, we watched Joseph park his truck alongside us. His truck was older than the señora's, with lots of dents in it. In some places, the colors were red and grey. Where the dents were on the truck, grey paint covered them.

Joseph's truck looked a lot like Papá's, the truck of a working man. No fancy truck with four doors and spikey hub caps; those were the trucks of men who sold drugs and people, riding through the towns of Mexico, promising girls manicures, pretty clothes, if they'd get into their trucks. I felt sad, then, thinking of those men and remembering Katia. I'd never understand why. My life would always carry the sadness of my friend, betrayed and murdered by demons. It would be very hard to trust another man again, a stranger outside of my family. I looked at Joseph sitting in his truck beside me, rolling his window down to speak to the señora. He smiled at me. His eyes were kind, like hers.

When they finished talking in English, Joseph got in the passenger side next to me. He took a pistol out of his boot and placed it on his lap.

I didn't like that. Nobody I knew carried a pistol, except for Ricky, Aamon, and Tomas. My father had a rifle. He told me pistols were for killing people, where a rifle was for shooting deer and turkey, animals to feed your family.

I would have to trust him, like I trusted the señora. It would take time. I knew her so much better than him. Sitting between them, I kept my eyes on the road in front of me. With no radio playing and no one talking or laughing, the day felt very long already, yet the morning sun was low in the cloudless blue sky. Once the señora had driven out of town, Joseph asked me about my family.

"*Eres la hija mayor?*"

I just nodded my head yes, all the while thinking about my responsibilities as the oldest child in my family, getting my brother ready for school, wiping the sleep from little Alicia's eyes. When evening came, I'd help Mama with cooking, then feed our dog the leftovers. I closed my eyes, creating little pictures in my mind of what they looked like, wondering if they thought I ran away because I didn't love them. *They took me! Demons stole me from all of you!*

Joseph kept staring at me, waiting for me to answer him, besides just the nodding of my head for yes. I didn't want to talk. I just wanted to ride in this truck until I was home.

"Ariela, esta bien, no estes triste."

I didn't need him to say I shouldn't be sad. I'd be sad for the rest of my life. The happy girl I was in Zaragoza didn't exist anymore. I didn't smile up at him; no, I wouldn't make him feel better for saying that. He waited for me to say something, then turned on the radio to fill the truck with noise.

The roads became smaller, no cars or trucks passing, no little stores to get gas and cold drinks. That's when I sat up taller in the bench seat and looked in the rearview mirror. I looked and looked, because I knew there were demons out there, hiding in the shadows, wanting to hurt me and my family.

CHAPTER TWENTY-FIVE

Miguel Avila
Wayside Drive
Houston, Texas

I got the one phone call from Tomas, then he stopped picking up, so I called El Jefe on one of the burners I kept stashed under the front seat of the car.

"Tomas isn't answering his phone, boss. I'm on my way to Rocksprings now. Some little shithole of a town west of San Antonio. I understand he had two girls with him."

"The idiot's dead, so is one of the girls. Don't know who did it. Find out. Get the other girl to Houston. Can't take a total loss on the investment. I got people waiting."

"I'll fix it."

"Is ICE still on your trail?"

"No, sir. I'll be in central Texas in a few hours. I got this."

I hung up and destroyed the burner, hitting it hard against the dashboard until the plastic pieces flew into the AC ducts and floorboard. Yeah, El Jefe was pissed, even worried about ICE. How the hell was I supposed to know if ICE was following me? But I didn't tell the boss that. I told him what he wanted to hear. I was the Fix-It Man, working both sides of the border, cleaning and disposing of jobs gone wrong.

It was already stinking hot in Houston, nothing but concrete here, not a breath of wind or shade to make it easier. I took my time before making the next phone call, smoking a cigarette, watching the women push shopping carts full of screaming kids in and out of Super Mercado.

If I planned this right, I'd still have time to get some girls in shape before the NBA playoffs next week. Lots of rich men were flying into town, wanting to party with the ladies and do some gambling on their favorite team. Tomas and his idiots cut it close for all of us with the botched job in Rocksprings. El Jefe didn't like losing money or making customers upset. I wasn't blood, and I wasn't even Mexican, so he'd just as soon kill me if I didn't straighten this shit out. The only thing I had going for me is I could speak both languages. That didn't make me a genius, just a spicy cracker. That's what El Jefe called me and my brother Luis the first time he met us and figured out our story. He laughed, repeating spicy cracker over and over, letting me know that's the pedigree I was with a white prostitute mama and a Mexican dealer papá. Spicy cracker—the only two people who didn't think those words were funny were me and Luis.

The boss man paid me well, so let him have his little joke. He was a paycheck to me, that's all, which was why I was sweating my cojones off in Houston, thinking central Texas was the last place I wanted to be, but I'd go, just like I've gone every time he asked. When El Jefe wanted to know what happened to his investments, I went. I smoked another cigarette, threw it out the window, and walked into the store for a twelve pack of beer for the ride. I could stay the night with Luis in San Antonio. He was always happy to share his weed and couch.

Luis and I were pretty much on our own since about fourteen or so. Our mother hadn't been around since we were little boys, still peeing in our pants. Nobody went looking for her either; after a while, no one mentioned her, much less the fact she left her two babies behind and never came back for them.

We lived with my dad's family on and off, an aunt in El Campo, our tiny abuela in Corpus Christi, an uncle in Victoria. Sometimes we even lived with the old man, but that didn't last longer than a weekend at the most, at least until he could find somewhere else to dump us off.

There were two things in our childhood Luis and me could count on: Christmas and Easter. Our old man playing Santa, flush with cash, always bought us new bikes or the latest Atari. By the time spring and Easter rolled around, he'd pop into our lives again, delivering two giant chocolate bunnies with hundred-dollar bills taped to the packages.

By the time Luis and I hit junior high, Aunt Rosa, tiny Abuela, and Uncle Tony were either dead or over us. The old man was in Huntsville,

serving life without parole for killing a DEA agent. My brother and I figured out how to take care of each other, making good money in Houston
as couriers and mules. We split up over the years because of women and
jobs, but we never stopped talking to each other. He was my little brother,
the one who took the short bus every day, still sounding out words when he
read his arrest warrants and parole violations. Funny, no matter how many
years went by, I still felt responsible for him.

Maybe Luis would ride out to Rocksprings with me, make a little extra
cash, help me out if things got weird. I threw a bag of barbeque-flavored
pork rinds into the shopping cart—they always went down good with
beer—and grabbed two Mexican rainbow coconut bars, knowing they'd
make Luis smile. My last purchase was at the register when I asked the
cashier to give me two cartons of Marlboro Menthols. Seemed crazy you
had to keep cigarettes under lock and key these days.

I was on I-10 West two hours before rush-hour traffic. When I stopped
in Sealy for gas, I reached under the car seat, searching for a burner. I had
five left, so I had to tighten this job up soon. I sent Luis a text I was on
my way. He texted back a new address, 3411 Seabreeze, around the I-410
S East Loop of San Antonio. I wasn't surprised by the new address. Luis
didn't stay in one place long, whether it was being short on rent or hiding
from a crazy-ass girlfriend, that's just the way he rolled. At least he was
smart enough to let me know before he changed phone numbers.

My next call was to an ICE agent El Jefe kept on payroll. Charlie
Bellows never rose through the ranks at the San Antonio office simply
because of his stupidity, but he did excel as an informant for me. He was an
unlikeable man, so you never had to worry about leaks. People just couldn't
stand him, whether it was his coworkers at ICE or the San Antonio police.

I'd been gleaning information from Charlie for about five years. And
for five years, I'd been paying him $500 cash for it. Yeah, Charlie was
stupid and very predictable. He always picked up on the second ring when
I called him.

"Hey man, can you talk?"

"I'll call you back in a second."

Just as I predicted, he did in five minutes. Of course, the first thing I
heard on the other end was him inhaling the first rush of nicotine from a

cigarette, then sucking the filter from his fat lips. Why he couldn't do that before he called, I never figured out. He was just a sorry Charlie. I laughed out loud thinking what a clown he was.

"What's so funny, man?"

"Nothing. Thought about something that happened earlier. I got a little trouble west of San Antonio in a town called Rocksprings. Tomas was working on some stuff for us there. Last word I got he was in this town when things fell apart. He's not picking up on his cell. Not answering texts. Nada. Boss man thinks he's dead. Maybe a girl who was travelling with him is dead, too. I need you to get me some information, maybe some names of people in the town."

"Sure. How you gonna pay me?"

"Look, Charlie. I'll pay you the way I always pay you, but I want the information first. Same way we've always done it."

I could almost hear his mind turning on the other end. At times I wanted to bash his head in with a baseball bat because he aggravated the hell out of me, but I was paid to be a patient man; otherwise, I wouldn't be a man in charge. I'd be a stupid thug like the rest of 'em.

"Give me a couple of hours."

"I'm on my way to San Antonio right now. We can meet once you've done your job."

"I'll call you with a meeting place, Miguel, but I'm not giving information on the phone."

"Yeah, that's usually how it works, Charlie."

I hung up and opened another can of beer while dodging eighteen-wheelers on I-10.

A few hours later I was parked in front of a row of caca boxes, little turds bunched up together on a street, accessorized with black iron burglar bars on every window. Probably built in the midsixties as a promising new subdivision for the working man and his family. True, it wasn't much of a dream home even when it was new, those 1,300 square feet with one bathroom, three bedrooms for six to eight people. But one thing I learned being yanked up as a kid across the Texas landscape is that one man's dream is another man's nightmare, and it always depended on your cash flow and who you worked for.

True to my little brother's taste, he found the worst neighborhood in San Antonio to live in, Dellcrest Forrest. The only thing slightly tropic at 3411 Seabreeze was an overgrown chinaberry tree covering up the front door. Most of the lawn was dead, with big ruts probably made from years of people parking in the yard. Today, a late model SUV without hubcaps sat underneath the chinaberry tree. The few patches of grass still living were near the deflated kiddie pool on the side of the house; a water hose snaked from somewhere in the backyard to the lip of the pool.

I sat in the car, sending my brother a text, asking him to meet me out front. I liked to assess any new situation before walking into it, especially where Luis was concerned. He'd always been a poor judge of character. That's what made him a thug and not a fix-it man.

A few minutes later, there he was, tall and skinny Luis, a spicy cracker living with a new set of people, including kids with a swimming pool. I hoped to God the kids weren't his, or better yet, a new girlfriend's kids. He was wearing the same Star Wars Jedi tee shirt I saw him in the last time I visited. Looked to be the same jeans, too, with a blow-out in the right knee. It was almost seven p.m., and the guy looked like he just rolled out of bed.

"Hey, man, come on in."

I walked toward him, carrying a plastic grocery bag with cigarettes, candy, a few cans of beer, and what was left of the barbeque pork rinds.

I gave him a hug and followed him into the living room with three couches pointed in the direction of a big screen TV with PlayStation cords connecting a skinny white chick on one of the couches. Two little kids in diapers were eating Cheerios out of a box at the feet of the white chick. One Mexican dude was asleep on the red couch near the white chick, so I chose to sit on the green plaid couch, as far away from them as I could. Luis sat down next to me.

"Sheila, meet my big brother, Miguel."

Sheila smiled at me, then bent over one of the kids on the floor, sticking her index finger in the back of his diaper. "You're good for another hour or two, Jo Jo."

She went back to playing Astro BOT. Nobody was talking. I guess they didn't want to wake up the man on the coach, so I took a cigarette out, offered one to Luis, and walked back out the front door.

"Luis, who are these people?"

"Sheila's with Carlos, the man on the couch. The two boys are hers. I was doing some work for them, and they offered me a place to stay."

"Is it cool for me to sleep here?"

"Yeah. Take my bed. I'll sleep on the coach. Kids usually get up early, but that don't bother me none."

He tugged on his cigarette, eyeing me, wondering why I was here.

"Want to get something to eat? I'm jonesing for a brisket sandwich with potato salad." I handed Luis a beer from my plastic bag.

"Yeah, let's go to the B&D Icehouse on Alamo. We can eat outside. There's always a chill crowd there. Live music."

We got back in the car and drove downtown. Just before we parked, Luis downed his beer and threw it out the car window. Messy. Always had been. Maybe I shouldn't take him to Rocksprings.

I handed him a hundred for the food and beer as he trotted off to wait in line. I sat down at a table etched in penknifed initials and checked my phone for texts. Charlie did his job. He wanted to meet tonight in front of the Menger Hotel. Good place. There'd be plenty of tourists walking around, drunk off overpriced margaritas and tacos from the River Walk. They'd stumble around the area for the rest of the night, looking for the perfect place to take a selfie.

Luis returned with the food and beer, sitting directly in front of me so I could get a view of him eating and talking at the same time. When his spittle landed in the potato salad, I made my decision. I didn't need his sloppy shit in Rocksprings. Enough idiots were already involved. This reunion would end with me dropping him off in front of the crack house he was sharing with those other slobs. That was always the difference between me and them. I might have been a spicy cracker, but I had a brain. It was the division between the thug and the professional.

Without much as far as a neck, or even legs, I imagined it was hard for Charlie to walk through life with confidence. He had the body shape of a pear, but it was his own choosing. A diet of beer and Big Macs was written on his swollen gut. I saw him outside the Menger Hotel, leaning against the cast iron lamp poles, looking sheepish and scared. How many more years would I have to deal with this fool?

He finally made eye contact with me when I was a few feet away. I nodded and walked toward the grounds of the Alamo. Like an obedient lapdog, he followed. Away from the landscaping lights, I waited in the shadow beneath the low-lying limbs of a live oak. The more I kept Charlie out of the light and from earshot, the easier my job would be.

"There's a hell of a mess in Rocksprings with border patrol and a murdered girl, illegal, found in a motel there," Charlie mumbled to me.

"So I hear."

"Got the same hard-ass sheriff in that county for years. Hoffman's his name. He won't budge or talk, so don't waste your time. You can get what you want from Marty Smith, border agent on the take for years. This is his personal cell."

He handed me a piece of paper. I looked up, scanning the scenery, then handed him a small paper bag, the size you kept a beer can in when you didn't have a koozie. Same size you used to get penny candy in if you'd been a good boy. He opened the bag, like I knew he would. It took everything in me not to stab that gut of his, but I walked away, didn't turn around once when the idiot kept calling my name.

"How do I know all the money is in here? Miguel, you hear me? Miguel?"

I lit a cigarette, smiling to myself as I walked among the tourists, drunk and spending more money than they had. Yeah, one man's dream is another man's nightmare, depending on what you had in your wallet and who you worked for.

I drove to Rocksprings, stopping at the H-E-B in Kerrville for beer, beef jerky, and string cheese. I gave Marty a call when I popped the top on the second one, right outside of city limits.

"What's the name of that motel in Rocksprings where the wetback was killed?"

"Who is this?"

"I'm your friend, Marty, the man who's gonna pay you good cash for being a crooked border agent."

"You know Charlie?"

"Yep."

"The Big Buck Motel. You can't miss it, on the main road, running through town."

"Arrest anyone?"

"Hell no, although another dead Mexican showed up, shortly after the motel killing. He was killed on a ranch outside of town. He's probably an illegal, like the girl. Sheriff thinks he murdered the girl in the motel before he got out to the ranch. Can't ask him any more questions, though. I do know the man was shot in the face, multiple body wounds with a rifle. Killed by the old woman who owns the ranch."

"Damn. Who's the old woman, Marty?"

"Hannah Durand. Don't bother looking for her. She's been missing since this morning, along with a Mexican girl we think was travelling with the murdered girl from the motel. Sheriff is out now, looking for leads."

"That sheriff's a regular Sherlock Holmes."

"How do I get my money?"

"¿Que?"

"Smart ass. I'll shoot you the minute you get to town, bury you out in the middle of nowhere. Nobody would find you, because nobody would go looking. No one cares when someone like you dies. The world just sighs with relief."

"No, you won't, Marty. I'll be long gone before you even figure out what I look like."

I hung up on Marty and finished beer number two. The farther I drove out of Kerrville, the more desolate the country became. I had another sixty miles to go on I-10 West, with not much traffic on the road except for eighteen-wheelers rising up and down the limestone hills, pushing eighty-five miles an hour. I popped the top on beer number three, thinking of the best way to clean up this mess.

There'd be no need to bully the sheriff. It would be best if the profile we had in Rocksprings disappeared, along with untraceable Tomas, just another dead illegal on the wrong side of the border. What I couldn't figure out was how important the other girl was to El Jefe. She was probably en route to Zaragoza for a big old family reunion. Why the old woman would want to drive her there was interesting. But those good Samaritans were always the same, thinking they got protection from God or earned a gold crown in heaven for their good deed. Reality was, in the godless land on the border, Good Samaritans end up dead.

If that little band of Jesus freaks left Rocksprings this morning, they were already in Mexico, enjoying the scenery. I'd put Ricky and Aamon back on the job. They knew the town and the girl. We didn't need any old lady or Mexican girl being heroes in Zaragoza. They'd be dead examples of why you should keep your mouth shut and mind your own business. El Jefe would like that.

I made it to the Garvin Store, at the corner of Highway 41 and 83, so I could pee. Beer always goes right through me, especially the older I get. It was a strange setup here, with the bathrooms outside the store, two little boxes covered in galvanized tin. I dodged a few weird peacocks roosting on a lopsided picnic table on the side of the store. It wasn't much of a driveway either, a few rocks and a lot of potholes.

I went into the store to get a Coke for the caffeine, and some woman behind the register started yapping to me about the honey and jewelry she made. Like I was gonna buy that crap. I put two dollar bills on the counter and walked out the door with my can of Coke. The whole place gave me the creeps, with bags of chips covered in dust on a wire rack and half-melted chocolate bars for sale by the register. Someone should have set fire to this ghetto convenience store a long time ago and put the crazy hippy chick and her weird peacocks in a cage, throwing away the key for good. The sooner I got back, the better I'd feel. This place made Houston look like a tropical paradise.

I lit a cigarette and opened all the car windows. With dry, hot air in my face and the first pull of nicotine in my blood stream, I called El Jefe. Of course, he liked my idea. That's why I get paid a lot, and why I'm still alive. I'm not sloppy, like the crooked cops, crack heads, and old hippies. I jerked the car out of the chuck holes and gravel of the Garvin Store and headed north on Highway 83 toward I-10. It was one of the few times in my life I was excited about getting back to Houston.

CHAPTER TWENTY-SIX

Border Agent Victor Cruz

Edwards County Sheriff Office
Rocksprings, Texas

It was impossible to take Sheriff Hoffman seriously with his teeth coated in orange cheese from the puffs he popped in his mouth while talking nonstop. True, it was somewhat of an accomplished feat, the ability to eat and talk so much without choking, but the visual was defeating, especially first thing in the morning.

When he asked me into his office to plan the next step, I hesitated. The man's truck, body, and clothes were a disgrace to the badge he wore. I expected no less in his office, and that's what I got.

His dog slept on a blanket under his desk. When Hoffman sat down, he kept referring to Butch while looking at his feet. The man was simply amazing when it came to protocol, but I kept my mouth shut. Patience and silence were the best ways to handle him.

While Hoffman continued to eat cheese puffs and talk to Butch, I checked my notebook. I'd already put in a call to ICE about gangs and cartel operating in Zaragoza. The results came quickly. I had an ID on the dead man at Durand Ranch and one on the murdered girl at the motel. The cartel from the Zaragoza area dealt in synthetic oxycontin, heroin, and human trafficking. There was a small weed trade, as well. It was too late to do anything on this side of the border. Besides, time was wasting. I knew where Hannah, Joseph, and Ariela were. They were on their way to Zaragoza. If I could get Hoffman to stop talking and eating, we'd get some work done.

Looked like he finally was coming up for air when he reached for the cup of coffee on his desk.

"Sheriff, this is the information I received from ICE." I placed the information in front of him, pushing the bag of cheese puffs to the side with the edge of the folder.

I allowed him time to read while I surveyed his office. He had a Western mount of a blackbuck next to a European mount of an axis deer with spider webs connecting the antlers. I wondered why he chose two completely different looks. Probably the work of that mother and daughter taxidermy team in Junction, who also rented U-Haul trailers. This was a strange area in Texas. People seemed to do what they wanted, no matter the rules, protocol, or laws.

There wasn't much rhyme or reason behind Hoffman, either. A methodological approach to a problem just wasn't in his DNA. The man was so arrogant, he actually counted on gut instinct. Of course, I knew what he thought of me—career federal law enforcer, overpaid clock-sucker with zero instinct. After all, he had to be voted into office. Looking at his constituents, I'm sure he picked up a lot of tabs at the local restaurants and contributed checks to the Rotary and high school football boosters for every vote he got. But everything is relative, even in Rocksprings, Texas.

He slammed the folder down on his desk after reading the report. No small moves for the mighty Sheriff Hoffman, but at least he wasn't reaching for the bag of cheese puffs before speaking.

"Hell, Hannah and Joseph are long gone with that girl. It's too late to stop anything here."

"Yes. I think it's best we work with authorities in Mexico and at the border. I've got some calls in."

"You could have talked to me first before calling them."

"Sheriff, this is out of your jurisdiction. I'm simply being a professional by sharing this information."

"Well, aren't you something, Cruz. You get a star and a cookie for being a border agent with manners."

I didn't say anything in return. I wasn't going to argue with him. His face was red with the veins in his neck pulsating to his increased heart rate. He popped a cheese puff into his mouth and stood up.

"I've known Joseph since I was a kid. Hannah, almost as long. I'm going to get them home safely. Whether it's officially my job or not. I know how to drive to Mexico. Been doing it all my life, while you were playing basketball in the driveway of some Dallas suburb."

He picked up his truck keys, grabbed two rifles and a box of shells from a cabinet near his desk, and walked out the door. The only reason I followed him was I thought he'd get everyone killed, including himself, with his Boy Scout bravado.

Before he slammed the front door to the dusty compound he presided over, he barked an order to the equally dusty secretary, Dolores.

"Taking the day, maybe tomorrow off. Take care of the dog. Give my wife a call."

Dolores wrote what he said on a rainbow-colored assortment of sticky notes, pasting two notes to the front of her computer monitor. Why she had to write them down as separate tasks to perform, let alone as a reminder to do, was bewildering. When she was writing, she nodded at Hoffman, then popped a handful of Milk Duds into her mouth. Unlike her boss, she closed her mouth while chewing, then washed it down with a huge gulp from a Mountain Dew can. *These people never stopped eating and drinking.*

I didn't get a nod from Dolores before we walked out the door. I got a go-to-hell look, which I returned with a nod of recognition. Hoffman and I left her among the clutter of candy boxes, sticky pads, and dust.

"I guess you think you're coming with me."

"Yes," I replied, opening the passenger side of his truck.

"Just keep your arrogant mouth shut, Cruz."

"Sheriff, I usually do, but one question I have to ask is how do you think you're getting into Mexico with those Texas plates and a sheriff's badge? Yes, I realize you visited Boy's Town when you were a kid."

"Never had a problem before, but now that I got you riding shotgun, Secret Agent Man, I thought you'd make some phone calls. Hit that easy button, government employee. Guys like you are used to taking the easy way out."

"I did that. I alerted the federales in Zaragoza with the ID of Hannah's truck and the name of Ariela's family. They'll need to get them to a safe place before that gang connects all the dots. They'll take out the family, all of them, as a way of showing strength. The last word they want on the streets is an old woman in Texas killed a gang member."

"Aren't you something, Cruz."

"Stop by the border patrol office on our way out of town, and we'll get the Mexican plates for your truck. Pick up a few more weapons."

Hoffman started the truck with full throttle, squealed his wheels in the parking lot, and sent a spray of gravel hitting the entrance to the Edwards County Sheriff's Office. The man was a jerk.

CHAPTER TWENTY-SEVEN

Padre Sánchez

Zaragoza, Mexico
Holy Angels Catholic Church
April 16, Feast of St. Bernadette of Lourdes

I was sweeping the front of the church steps when I saw the truck. The same truck that drove away with Ariela and Katia. Red, double cab, big tires, a truck driven either by rich Tejanos or the cartel. *Dios tenga misericordia.* The poor mothers who suffered for the carelessness of their daughters never stopped praying at the church, coming at all hours, knees bent, wails between prayers, begging Madre Maria to intercede for the safe return of Ariela and Katia.

Katia was a disobedient child from the day she was born, but Ariela wasn't. She came from a good family, but her mistake was being a follower, a follower of Katia. She paid dearly for it. Everyone knew they were dead or part of the sex trade in Houston, soon to be sold to someone who would put them on airplanes, shipping them off like animals to a market run by Godless men and women. It would be easier for these poor mothers to accept their death, rather than the daily horror of imagining where their daughters were and what evil surrounded them.

I watched the same red truck that brought sadness to these families sit idle underneath the little oak tree in the courtyard. Inside were Ricky and the strange-looking man who was with him last time he came to Zaragoza. After the shock of seeing them, I wondered why they were here. To steal more of our girls? To recruit our boys into a life of sin with the gifts of a cell phone and American money?

I walked back to the church office and called the *policia*. Eduardo Campos, the philistine of justice in Zaragoza, answered. When I told him what I saw, he gave me the same reply he always gave, "I will look into this, Padre." The man was a filthy liar. His waddling ass rarely did any work for the people of this town, except if he could personally profit.

I returned to the chapel, kneeling in front of the sanctuary, the physical presence of God exposed in the opened tabernacle of the Eucharist. The holy of the holies. And I believed, despite the crimes of the Church, because I had no choice. To not accept the profound truth made my life meaningless.

I had little time for my own thoughts, as the parishioners would soon fill the pews, seeking resolution and paying reverence to Saint Bernadette of Lourdes, the little French girl no one believed, especially the clergy of the Church. "The crazy peasant girl." *Mujer loca.* The clergy of France, shepherds to the flock, despised her persistence, calling her names, refusing to believe Mother Mary, even angels would speak to a female, poor and ignorant, a dirty little sheep. Years later, after the investigations, the Church changed its mind, as it often did, and renamed the crazy peasant girl Saint Bernadette. Around the world, people praised her on her feast day.

But the Church had to be careful! It couldn't always believe what these visionaries said; there may be mental illness or a need for attention, or even vanity, the greatest sin of women. These women, even young girls always saying, "Look at me, look at me, aren't I beautiful?" Oh, they didn't have to ask for attention with loud voices, they were shrewd and deceptive, making men notice them with their tight clothes, high heels, and faces full of makeup. Katia was a perfect example of this kind of behavior. I spent hours telling her modesty was a virtue to be admired, but she knew better, even taunted me with winks and smiles. *Triste, triste.* Sadly, she was punished for her vanity and rebellion, knowingly getting into the red truck with sex traffickers. Ricky most likely dangled a few American dollars or a cheap necklace in front of those eyes, and she grabbed it, never thinking she wouldn't see her poor mother again.

Sí, on St. Bernadette's feast day, perhaps a miracle would occur, and the lost girls of Zaragoza, our Katia and Ariela, would be returned safely to their homes and families. When I uttered their names in prayer, the smell of roses filled the sanctuary. I opened my eyes and quickly glanced around the church, thinking someone had entered. Maybe one of the women with the Altar Society, bringing flowers for Mass. But there was no one, only the silence of the icons. Then the flickering of flames appeared before me. I moved toward its glow, where the portrait of Our Lady of Guadalupe hung near the south transept. The tiny flames came from the portrait of Mary, her green cape of gold-colored stars glowing, pulsating in the heat. When I gained the nerve to come closer to her portrait, the faces of Ariela and Katia appeared within each star of Mary's cape. *Santa María, Madre de Dios.*

I fell to my knees, lowering my head, singing the words I have sung to her throughout my life, as her faithful servant, *"Ave María! ¡Dulce doncella! Oh, escucha la oración de una doncella. Porque tú puedes oír entre lo salvaje . . ."*

I raised my head to dry my eyes on the sleeves of my vestige, only to see the flaming stars extinguished. She was gone! I approached the portrait slowly, a mixture of fear and hope within me, as hundreds of questions clouded my head, wondering if she would appear, again. Oh, how my life would change! This broken church, as dust filled as this miserable town, would become an official site of a Marian Apparition. The people. The money. Finally, I would be welcomed in Rome.

When I stood in front of the portrait, searching into the eyes of Santa Maria, nothing was there. Cold, lifeless art. The smell of roses was gone, as well. Estupido! Then, I knew what the vision meant. It was a call to renew my faith, and I remembered the words of St. Paul, "For we live by faith, not by sight." I accepted the mystery of faith, just as I did God's unanswered prayers.

I returned to the business of preparing for Mass. It wasn't the first time God disappointed me, but I continued to work for Him. Why God rewarded some priests and not me was a mystery, like so many things in the Church. I walked into the sacristy for the surplice with its square collar, placing it over my head, wondering where the altar servers were. The children were always late, running in here with dirty tennis shoes and sweaty tee shirts, ungrateful to be serving in the house of God. The sheep were dirty, but I accepted that, too.

CHAPTER TWENTY-EIGHT

Eduardo Campos
Chief of Police
Zaragoza, Mexico

Pissant priest! Ordering me around like I was one of his sheep. *Arrogante.* He knew better. I'm the Man in Zaragoza. While he dreamt of fondling altar servers, I was taking calls from border patrol agents and ICE. I did just what those Anglos wanted me to do, rounding up the white woman and man she was traveling with from Texas along with everyone in the Morales family, including the girl, Ariela. Just at daybreak, I picked them up, put them in the back of my truck, covered them with a plastic tarp, and drove out of town. They all complained, crying and whining how hot it was under the tarp, whimpering they couldn't breathe, but I kept the radio on full blast all the way out to the abandoned office at the Rosario Silver Company. I couldn't tolerate complainers.

As soon as I got to the Rosario mine, I tucked them away in a tin can trailer with no electricity, but they had bottled water, chips, and two candy bars if they got hungry. It's all I had in the office, but at least there'd be no whining about hunger. These were poor people; they were used to getting by on very little food and water.

I couldn't wait until the two Texas lawmen, big mucho heroes, would have to deal with the trailer and the people in it. I couldn't wait to see them all leave. Good riddance. No one invited them here, much less the old woman and the man she travelled with. Yes, I gave them credit for even attempting this. It was stupid, but it did show some guts, thinking they could avenge two Mexican girls abused by the cartel. They were no different than Padre Sánchez, all of them fools who believed their good deeds would be rewarded with a first-class ticket to heaven.

126

The man with the old woman reminded me of a banty rooster, all puffed up, ready for a cock fight. I guess he wanted to impress her, though she was too skinny and old for my taste. No hips, breasts, not much of a woman. I don't know what he saw in her. He was a much younger man, handsome, in good shape. The entire scenario was *ridículo*. I had no hope any of it would work as far as saving the girl and her family. I didn't care. I'd get my money either way.

The Texans were armed. Ruben Morales brought a rusted rifle he hadn't fired in decades. It was hard not to laugh in the stupid peasant's face. I warned them all to keep quiet and stay in the trailer until I came back with Cruz and Hoffman. I hoped the sheriff had enough brains to take them all back across the border. If any of them stayed, Ruben, his wife, and the children, they'd all be shot by the cartel. There was no use talking to Sylvia Hernández. Her daughter was dead. I'd wait until this blew over before I'd let her know.

I'd get some gringo cash for my trouble, but it was never enough to risk death for being a hero. El Jefe's boys would chop me up with a machete in broad daylight. Let the stray dogs in town eat what was left of me, making a strong example of what happens to traitors in Zaragoza. I predicted things would get uglier, and I wasn't saving any of these fools but myself.

I've dealt with a few border agents in my time, but Cruz was different. For one thing he spoke Spanish, like the Texan with the old lady. Lover boy never spoke Spanish to me, but I heard him comforting Ariela and her father before I left the trailer. All the hero talk gave me a big headache and made me tired. The gringos in the trailer were predictable, but Cruz was hard to read.

I know the money he'd offered wouldn't be like ICE, but it was better than nothing. Agencies, organizations, don't impress me much. It didn't matter if it was ICE, the Church, or the cartel. After a while, they were all transparent—all about money and power. Once I guessed the game, it wasn't so interesting anymore. That's why I wasn't surprised Ricky and Aamon were back in town. El Jefe sent them here to clean up the mess. I laughed my ass off thinking how that old woman from Texas killed a member of El Jefe's gang.

I should ride around town and look for them, maybe get some food at the Chicken Man taquería, see if Ricky and Aamon were there, but my intervention would be nada. It was best to ignore them, like I didn't know what was going on. I was hoping Cruz and Hoffman wouldn't act like vigilante Texans lighting up the sky with their guns, showing their stupid bravery in a town the cartel fed.

I locked the office door and drove a block to the taquería. The owners, Michael and his sister Veronica, were sweating most of the day over a used oil barrel with a grill over its opening. The tacos de guisadas were my usual choice. Veronica had a plastic folding table with bowls of sauces, hard-boiled eggs, rice, and limes. All of it was fresh except the limes, too sour. They always had brown around the edges. Rotten.

Michael cooked rellena, chicharron, picadillo, chicken livers, and chile rellenos. You made your choice, and he placed the grilled meat in a corn tortilla Veronica made with her two little hands. Some days I got the boiled eggs, especially if my gut was bad and needed to be filled with bland foods. Other times I'd go to the Chicken Man and talk to Veronica, watching closely as the sweat dripped from her neck into the small hollow between her breasts.

"*Que paso*, Michael. Two chile rellenos," I ordered without placing any money on the plastic table Veronica stood behind. They knew better than to ask for money. Veronica pushed a paper napkin of chopped onions in my direction.

I ate the chile rellenos standing in front of them. Neither one would make eye contact.

"Veronica, let's see those big bedroom eyes." I reached out and touched her chin, moving her face closer to mine. Michael looked at me once, then returned to his oil barrel, stoking the fire, then placing a beef shank on the grill with a long-handled fork. The fat from the beef popped in the flames below. He'd better keep his eye on it, or that cheap cut of meat would be stringy and tough.

"Have you seen Ricky Alvarez in town? I'm talking to you, Michael."

I moved my hand from Veronica's face to her right breast.

"I haven't seen Ricky in years. Don't know if he's even alive," Michael replied, staring at my hand on his sister's breast. I could almost hear his heart pounding from where I stood.

"Call me if you see him," I said, moving my hand from Veronica's breast and slapping her on the ass. "Thanks for the food, amigo."

I wasn't back in my office more than a few minutes when Cruz and the sheriff showed up. When I opened the door to let them in, Ricky Alvarez rode by in his red truck and shot me the finger. Michael probably called him after I left, sold me out for one thousand pesos or less. *Damn you, Chicken Man. I'll kill you, dump your lifeless body into the hot oil barrel you cook on, until you're nothing but ash and bone.*

Ricky and the skeleton riding shotgun with him saw Cruz and Hoffman. They knew who they were without the Texans wearing a uniform or a badge. I knew they'd follow us out to the silver mine. Getting the Texans and the Morales family out of the trailer would cost a lot of blood. It wasn't going to be mine.

CHAPTER TWENTY-NINE

Ariela

Zaragoza, Mexico

The policia, Señor Campos, came to our house early in the morning, even before breakfast. I heard his truck door slam shut when the sun was barely awake in the sky, stretching its arms wide across the horizon, bringing the first rays of light. The rooster on Papá's truck hood stood proudly, singing his song, followed by the chorus of three white-winged doves nestled in the mesquite tree behind the house. The world was awake and watching when Señor Campos approached our front door.

Señora Hannah and Joseph were the first to hear his knocking. They'd been sleeping in the living room with the señora resting on the couch and Joseph sitting nearby in Papá's overstuffed chair. I came quickly with my parents when I heard the footsteps on the porch. The innocents slept through it, Javier and Alicia, cuddled together in the twin bed at the back of the house.

My father opened the door to Señor Campos, with Mama, Señora Hannah, and Joseph standing behind him. I stood next to Papá. I wasn't afraid when he was beside me.

"Ariela, take your dog inside the house. Señor Campos, excuse the dog. She will not bite you, but she is doing her job, protecting the family."

"I don't have time for your mutt, much less your family, Ruben. I'm leaving in five minutes. If you and the others, including the gringos behind you, want to live another day, you'll get in the back of my truck and keep your mouths shut."

A small cry escaped from my mother's clenched fist covering her mouth. I turned away from her, so I wouldn't cry, too. Bolt sensed our fear and began barking, baring her teeth at Señor Campos, as the hair on the ridge of her back began rising, making her body appear larger against the enemy she saw in front of her. My fingers moved quickly, untying the knot in the rope holding her in place. I was afraid she'd choke herself if she kept lunging at Señor Campos, but I was most afraid of him kicking her with his pointy boots. I saw the weakness in his eyes and how he carried his body, bully man, bully policia, frightening the most tender hearts in his sight, Mama and Bolt. He was the type of man who would kill or maim a defenseless creature. I should know. I learned to smell, see, and taste evil the days I spent in hell with demons. I took Bolt into the house, as far away as I could from this demon on our porch.

She was a special animal, more than just a pet to me. I missed her when I was in Texas, but I knew she'd never forget me, whether I was on the other side of the border or not. She was smart and had spiritual powers, like the Aztec god Xolotl she was named for, the god who ruled over lighting and fire, guiding souls into the underworld when people died.

She had a sixth sense, too, a special instinct inside her. She knew Señor Campos was a bad man before any of us. Mama called her a guardian angel dog, a powerful little mutt with a solid black coat except for the white star right above her eyes. She might have been the ghost dog that protected me in Texas. A true guardian angel, she could travel all over the world, flying in the night above the earth, in her journey to protect those she was closest to.

I was so careful with her, knowing others would be jealous, wanting to steal her for her protective powers. I tied her to the porch post every time we went somewhere or even when we went to bed at night. Mama wouldn't let me keep her inside unless there was a storm.

We all protected and loved her in the family, but I was her special caretaker, feeding and playing with her more than anyone else.

When Señor Campos told me I couldn't take her to the silver mine where he was hiding us from the cartel, I cried. He said we wouldn't be there long, the men from Texas would come soon and help Joseph and Hannah get back home. He explained it as if in an hour or so, we would all be in our own homes again and life would return to what it was before I got into Ricky's truck.

I retied Bolt to the porch post, placing two little bowls of water and meat scraps next to her so she wouldn't hurt herself pulling the rope toward something too far away. Once I got home from the silver mine, I could take her for a walk, even play ball with her in the yard, but I was wrong to have that thought, as wrong as I had ever been in this nightmare I never could wake from.

Señor Campos put us in the back of his truck, even Hannah and Joseph. He grabbed Papá's rifle from him before he got in the truck, then he tried to take the pistol and rifle Hannah and Joseph brought. Joseph wouldn't let him.

"*No confío en ti*, Campos. *Voy a ir a Texas esta noche. Esta pistola hará que ese plan funcione.*"

Like me, Joseph thought this would all be over in a few hours. He and the señora would drive back to Texas and take care of the ranch and animals. I would go home with my family.

Señor Campos cursed quietly and gave Papá's rifle back to him. Then he told us to lie on our stomachs in the back of his truck. He covered us with a thick blanket of plastic. Javier and Alicia cried, "Too hot, too hot, we cannot breathe," but the truck did not stop for their cries. Papá thought we had been in the back of the truck for thirty minutes, until Señor Campos stopped, slammed the truck door closed, and lifted the plastic blanket from us. He told us to get out and into the little white trailer near the truck.

I looked around as I walked into the trailer. Yes, we were here, at the Rosario Silver Mine, the same mine where Katia's papá was buried alive, smothered by dirt and rocks. Señor Campos locked us in the white trailer and told us not to open the windows, talk, or even move from where we sat on the floor, beneath the silent air conditioner in the window. We had to listen. Listen hard for his return. He promised he'd be back for us, but he did not come in an hour, or even the "two hours at the most" he swore by.

CHAPTER THIRTY

Ricky

Zaragoza, Mexico

Viejo gordo, Eduardo Campos with your lard ass! There wasn't a man or woman in Zaragoza who wouldn't sell him out. He'd been pushing people around since he was the fat bully with the pimply face on the school playground. I got away with being a bully for the cartel because I offered cash and protection. His offerings, his promises—nada.

Since my cousin Veronica was in braids, he'd been touching her. It was at the point now that he did it in daylight at the Chicken Man in front of her brother. Michael, *siempre el niño de una mama*, still hiding behind an apron, like a weak mama's boy, couldn't do a thing about it except stand behind the oil barrel, cooking and fretting like a woman. He had no respect for himself, so why would Campos respect him?

Michael wasn't man enough to stop Campos, but I would. It would be easy to pull a trigger rested on his temple, then let Aamon do his magic with a machete. Aamon was ready for blood as soon as I drove into Zaragoza. No one would ever find the tiny pieces he'd leave behind of Eduardo, because no one would care to look.

When we saw him with the Texans, I kept our adrenaline pumping by driving out to the Morales house a mile out of town. It would be the first place the old white woman from Texas would bring Ariela. Home to her crying mama! Those foolish old women raised on piety and suffering for the Church—what did it get them? A house full of children they can't feed, strapped to a penniless man they can't divorce. My church was the cartel; the more I gave, the more I received.

For all their faith and penitence, the Moraleses' home was a cinder block cave in a grassless yard. A few scrawny chickens pecked in the dirt next to the old man's truck. Nobody was home, as far as I could tell. No kids running in the yard. No mamacita calling their names for beans and tortillas.

Aamon got out of the truck, sniffing around for people. I stayed behind, watching him circle the yard, walking in and out of the house, then kicking the mutt tied to the front porch post. Out of the corner of my eyes, I saw the old man. He probably lived next door. He was walking as fast as he could from his small garden in the back to the safety of his house. Carrying a single blade hoe with him, he leaned on it like a cane, dragging his right foot behind him. First thing I thought to myself was the old man better speed things up before Aamon saw him. *Vamos abuelo!* But the old man was too slow.

"*¿Dónde está Morales?*" Aamon screamed from the side of the house, just as the old man was about to make it to the back door. He didn't turn around when Aamon continued to call him, only dug the wooden handle of the hoe harder into the ground, launching himself into the safety of the door just within reach. He was almost there, pushing and dragging his crippled limb through the dirt, until he stopped, positioned the hoe against the door threshold, and pulled the doorknob. I admired him in a way. All the effort he showed, but it was useless, like a roach scrambling from one giant, black boot. Aamon called again.

"¿Dónde está Morales?"

You should answer him, old man! It will only be harder for you if you keep ignoring him. But it was too late. With one hand, Aamon reached for the old man's shoulders and pulled him to the ground. He picked up the hoe resting against the door and struck the tiny, grey head of the old man. Instinctively, the old man covered his skull with both hands. The hoe never stopped striking the hands and head in its path.

Then came the distinct sound of metal hitting bone and the softest murmur of "Silver mine."

Aamon got back in the truck with the brains of the old man splattered on his face, shirt, and jeans.

"Go back in the house and clean yourself off. Mierda, all over my truck, man."

Like the obedient, mad dog he was, Aamon walked back into the

Morales house. A few minutes later, I saw him bare chested, smoking a cigarette in front of a window near the porch. Taking the cigarette from his mouth, he touched the red eye of its tip to the cloth curtains. The dog tied on the porch post began jerking on its rope collar, barking at Aamon. He ignored it and got back in the truck.

"Let it burn. Let the whole town see it. They better learn what happens when you don't listen to what I say. Next is the old woman who drove the truck with Texas plates over here, thinking she was smart to hide it in the old man's yard."

I didn't look at him, only at the dog on the porch tied to the post. The higher the flames got, the higher the dog jumped, frantically trying to pull away from the rope anchoring him to the house.

"Damn, Aamon. Untie the dog. It didn't do anything." The soft spot in my gut spoke those words. It always did when I thought of my mother. How her life was like the dog's. Neither one of them ever had a chance.

Aamon removed the tee shirt he had sticking out of the back of his jeans and pulled it over his head. I guess it belonged to Ariela's father. Rueben Morales. I remembered him when I was a kid. Quiet man. Now, a homeless man. I looked over at Aamon to see if he heard what I said. When I leaned toward him, he reached across the truck and grabbed my throat, squeezing it until I began kicking my legs under the steering wheel and slapping his forearms to break his grip.

"You never stop talking, always telling me what to do. I'm the boss, now. Shut up and drive the truck."

We drove out to the silver mine in silence.

CHAPTER THIRTY-ONE

Border Agent Cruz
Zaragoza, Mexico

Campos was a dangerous man. We were in town less than five minutes when two cartel members drove by, recognizing our vehicle and us. The entire operation was doomed at that point. Hoffman knew it, too, and wasted no time letting Campos know.

"You're double dipping here, Campos. You can't serve two masters without getting someone killed, or hell, all of us killed."

"No hablo ingles. You're in Mexico now, gringo. You and Cruz need to speak Spanish."

"Ain't happening," Hoffman popped back, moving closer to where Campos was standing, giving him a quick jab in his protruding gut. "Putting a few pounds on, I see. That extra weight can slow a man down, but I guess you already know that."

"Take it easy, Hoffman. We don't have time for arguing. We've got to get to the mine and get those people out of there before the cartel shows up. Campos, we'll take your truck. I'm loading the .45 caliber and some soft body armor for us and two AR-15s. You'll need to supply yourself with a firearm. You're not touching ours."

Campos gave me a side look of disbelief; it could have been fear, but I wasn't going to hold his hand through the mess he created. It was easy for a man like Campos to bully his way around as the official lawman in Zaragoza, taking money and favors from all sides, never fearing repercussions, but he was in a different league now. I also knew he didn't want to drive, but I was giving the orders, here. Hoffman was too unpredictable with his hot-head emotions, and Campos couldn't be trusted.

With both hands on the steering wheel, Campos couldn't pull his pistol on me and Hoffman. It's also why I sat upfront, making sure those hands stayed on the wheel. Hoffman didn't have the patience to keep his mouth shut and watch the man, so he got in the back with the firearms. I made him think he was needed to secure the weapons.

I learned from my father a long time ago everybody needed a job and a role to play. It was the best management advice I received, despite all the training from the Feds. Dad knew he had to be one step ahead mentally to make it in the military as an enlisted Mexican man. On the government's goofy scale, he was one of the lowest paid, with little authority, despite his education. But he bided his time out at Carswell Field, patiently waiting for a promotion. He did it with his head down, working hard. He had no other choice as an American citizen, born in Texas but with Mexican skin. Those were the times and the hierarchy of the military. He found his role, and it was making every boss he had look good. Eventually, those promotions came, and we got a nice house in the suburbs of Dallas. My mom was finally happy, thinking white housewives were going to invite her over for coffee. They never did.

I respected my father for his work ethic and patience, but I couldn't do the military. I came into my job as a customs and border protection officer in San Antonio, working my way up, trying to secure entry ports as well as keeping agents safe. In time, I was burnt out from administrative work. The final knockout came when one of my off-duty agents was found dead in a motel room. A father to three kids still in school, Daniel Lopez was hog-tied and shot with a single bullet to the back of his head.

The stress mixed with depression eventually took its toll on my marriage, so I took a pay cut and got out of San Antonio, thinking Rocksprings would be slower paced, with low-key field work. I arrived one week before the murder of Katia Hernández.

I knew immediately what my job was here, and what role I needed to play. I'd never be the coconut most expected me to be in this uniform, brown-skin man acting white, betraying my culture. My father taught me to always think one step ahead of everybody else. I did. My job was to protect men, women, and children victimized by criminals on both sides of this border, regardless of their color or nationality. I kept my mouth shut about that, because words didn't matter in this game, only action.

Bad and good, legal and illegal, criminal and victim—it appeared to be black and white, but none of it was. You had to think beyond the obvious. Most of the time, I thought about everyone's next move before they realized they were out of options.

I rode shotgun next to Campos, making a small notation in my notebook of his truck's make and model. When cell service returned, I'd send a text back to the office, but the farther we drove toward the silver mine, the more I felt disconnected from the world. It was like falling off a cliff into nothingness.

"I don't know how you think that notebook of yours is going to help us," Hoffman said from the back seat.

"So far it's gotten us here without having our heads blown off."

"Some would call that a bonus day in police work."

Hoffman kept making wisecracks from the back seat, laughing at his own jokes. The man was easily amused. I was surprised he didn't bring the bag of cheese puffs he ate on the ride to Zaragoza. His appetite and unprofessionalism never stopped surprising me. I kept my eyes on Campos's hands on the steering wheel as he gripped it tighter and tighter, his knuckles white against the brown of his skin.

"Looks like we're in for some weather," Hoffman announced as lightning lit the sky in front of us.

He began counting one, one thousand and two, one thousand . . . When he reached six, one thousand, a boom of thunder sounded. I was ready to punch him—my nerves were shot.

"My dad taught me how to count the distance between lighting and thunder when I was a kid. That lighting is about six miles from us."

"Nice science lesson, Hoffman. Maybe we should focus on the job ahead of us."

"I figured out my job a long time ago, Cruz. My job is to not get killed."

"It will be an ambush. They're waiting for us there," Campos said.

Raindrops pelted the windshield as the sky turned purple, then burnt orange, finally black with the occasional flash of lighting. The wind increased, whipping small rocks from the shoulder of the road into the side panels of the truck. Campos slowed the truck down to avoid any damage to the windshield.

Between the dust from the road and the rain, it was hard to see anything out of the passenger window or the windshield. When Campos whispered, "Lechuza," I followed his gaze to a large black bird, bigger than an owl, sitting on top of a telephone pole near the shoulder. It was covered in long, black hair. I wasn't close enough to see the eyes or a beak.

"What's a Lechuza, Campos? It has to be the strangest bird I've ever seen."

Before he could reply, the bird swooped toward the front of the truck and looked at Campos; its facial features were that of an old woman with a twisted face.

"Madre Maria," Campos cried, making the sign of the cross against his body while driving the truck with one hand. The truck swerved to the right shoulder of burnt grass and rocks.

"Jesus, Campos. Get the truck on the road before the Lechuza comes back to gouge your eyes out," Hoffman yelled. "Cruz, that weird bird you saw is supposed to be a witch, a Lechuza, seeking revenge against men who have hurt women. Mexican folklore. Heard the tale even when I was a kid in Rocksprings."

"Sometimes a Lechuza can cause a thunderstorm," he went on. "Electricity is her magic. I've heard of Lechuzas chasing trucks out in the desert, only to short out their batteries, leaving the passengers stranded in the middle of nowhere. Looks like our friend here has got some bad mojo following him. What did you do to the women of Zaragoza, Campos?" Hoffman kicked the back of Campos's seat with his boot.

"*Callate*," Campos replied, never turning around to look at Hoffman and me. Shut up, he told us, as if we didn't know we were entering the gates of hell the closer to we got to the silver mine.

"See if you have any cell coverage, Hoffman. I'm not getting any bars out here. If you do, check the radar. Maybe this is a quick storm moving through and not a spell cast by a witch."

"I don't need a video weatherman to tell me what's happening outside. This is one of those supercell thunderstorms. They move through this time of year, between the end of spring and beginning of summer." Hoffman leaned into the back of my seat and lowered his voice. "We're in it for the long haul, Cruz. So sit back, because this is going to be the calmest part of your day. All hell's about to break loose here with hail, maybe some tornadoes. The only thing you can be sure of is as each moment passes by, the next moment will be worse. This little storm in front of you is nothing compared to what you'll get at the silver mine."

He started laughing, then kicked the back of Campos's seat, again.

"What do you think about that, Campos?"

Campos didn't flinch or say a word. He continued driving with both hands on the steering wheel, looking at the road straight in front of him. I had to give him credit for his focus. Regardless of Hoffman's mouth, Campos drove the truck with nerves-of-steel purpose, working toward his destination like he'd been waiting for this moment his entire miserable life.

CHAPTER THIRTY-TWO

Ariela

Rosario Silver Mine

Hail pelted the little trailer like bullets hitting a tin can.

"Target practice," Joseph whispered under his breath as he walked past me. I'm sure he didn't know I heard him or even understood his words, but I did. I kept those words inside me, where all my fears lived, jumpy and shaky, rattling like leaves in a windstorm, waiting for the moment all I knew and loved would be changed, gone forever. But I was a good secret keeper. Poker face is what Katia called me. Most of the time, no one knew what I really thought or felt. It was the only thing I could control in my life. No one could take my thoughts from me.

I sat on the floor beneath the little air conditioner silent in the window frame. Next to me sat Javier and Mama with baby Alicia on her lap, sleeping, although it was already so hot this early in the morning. It would only get worse the longer we waited in the airless little trailer. No one talked about how long that would be, but you knew everyone was thinking that, just by looking in their eyes.

Papá and Joseph were the only ones standing up, checking to see if the toilet flushed. It didn't. Next, they tried every light switch, up and down, up and down. No light. Nothing worked in here. The electricity was turned off a long time ago.

When the workers left this little trailer, the insects moved in. Tiny ants in single file marched silently along the plastic baseboards and floor seams, then around the dried carcasses of roaches and scorpions, in their search for water. In the corners of the window frames and along the ceiling, spider webs dropped the smallest white threads, connecting the spiders to the tiny bugs below. Maybe the spiders would be lucky when a fly or two flew straight into the webs. This was my view from the floor: the smallest of animals, tiny bugs, searching for food and water. Just like us, they were trying to survive.

We had water, though. Javier and Mama drank a plastic bottle each. Mama moistened her hand with some of her water, then rubbed it over Alicia's forehead and neck, through her hair matted against her face. But I saved mine. I wondered if I should share it with the tiny ants, making a little bowl for them out of the white plastic cap. Papá would be upset with me for wasting it, so I only looked at the bottle of water, telling myself not to open it until I couldn't stand the burning thirst in my throat anymore.

Señora Hannah and Joseph weren't drinking water, either. They sat close together, staring ahead at the door of the trailer with their pistol and rifle on their laps, smiling at us, listening hard for different sounds outside. Papá's old rifle leaned against the little air conditioner in the window.

We were all listening, concentrating so hard beads of sweat appeared on our foreheads and throats. The señora looked very tired, with a line of sweat above her upper lip like a little mustache. But she didn't complain, only kept smiling at me and Javier. I saw Joseph wipe the sweat off her mouth with the red handkerchief from his back pocket, but I quickly turned away, embarrassed for her.

Mama's fingers quickly touched each bead of her rosary as she whispered prayer after prayer, pleading for an intercession, begging for a miracle. When Alicia stirred in her lap, she rocked her back and forth to the rhythm of her prayers. But still no one came to rescue us from the long hours of heat and fear in the little trailer.

I was so tired, tired of concentrating on the ants, listening to Mama's breathy prayers, and staring at the plastic doorknob in front of me. The growing heat was like a suffocating blanket on my body, making my eye lids heavier and heavier. I wanted to sleep, so I could be away from the little trailer, but I couldn't. My parents and my little brother and sister might need me.

When I first heard the spray of gravel hit the front of the trailer, I thought I was dreaming. Then when I heard two truck doors slamming and men shouting, I remembered where I was and who was outside, waiting for us.

Joseph crawled to the window near the door, lifted the blinds at the bottom, and peered outside.

"It's a red truck. New. Two Mexican men with guns."

"It's Ricky and Aamon," I blurted.

Alicia was awake now, crying.

"Shh! Come here, here by me, and stay quiet. They don't know we're in here," Señora Hannah said to me. "*Dile a tu madre que calme al bebé.*"

I helped Mama with Alicia until she stopped crying, then I moved Javier closer to both of them. When everyone seemed calmer, I placed my head on the señora's lap, my heart pounding against her thigh. Listening, all of us straining our ears and eyes at the front door of the trailer. First came the sound of the men walking through the gravel, then we heard their boots on each step of the porch in front of the trailer door. Then the footsteps stopped. The sound of another truck pulled its way through the gravel. It came so close to the trailer, some of the rocks hit the front door.

"Get down, everyone. Flat on the floor. Don't make a sound, now. *Yacen planas,*" Joseph whispered to us. Lying on my stomach with my eyes closed tightly, I listened to the men outside. I held Javier's small, sweaty hand in mine with one hand and the señora's with the other. Papá and Mama were lying next to each other with Alicia in the middle, their arms covering her tiny body.

"*Baja el arma,* Ricky. Put it down."

It was the voice of Señor Campos. Then the first shot came, followed by many, until all I could hear were the bullets spraying the trailer and trucks. I put my hand over Javier's mouth, while Mama covered Alicia's, as we tried to smother their screams. Then silence, as frightening as the gun shots. I turned on my right side and saw Joseph crawling toward the door. Hannah pulled on his leg, mouthing "No, no." It didn't stop him. He stood up, turned the doorknob, and moved through the slit in the door.

"Hoffman. We're all in here. Hannah, Ariela, and her family."

"Glad to see you alive, Joseph. Now get back in the trailer until we clean this mess up."

The door closed and Joseph smiled at us, bending over to help Señora Hannah to her feet, then he reached for my mother's hand. Papá picked Alicia and Javier up and held them in his arms.

Joseph and the señora helped me up, together. She hugged me tightly and said in my ear, "*Los hombres malos están muertos*. All shot dead. Ariela, those men can never hurt you again, or any other girl. Campos is dead, too. We need to wait until the sheriff and Agent Cruz cover the bodies before we leave the trailer. It won't be much longer, now."

I understood almost every word she said, knowing the most important words were the demons were dead. I turned to my father and mother, my brother and sister, then walked slowly into their arms. I held them tightly, allowing myself to cry for all of us, but most of all, for Katia and her mother.

CHAPTER THIRTY-THREE

Hannah

Durand Ranch
Rocksprings, Texas

I have no doubt in my mind we broke a lot of laws bringing the Morales family back to the ranch. Those actions started the rumor mill again with the locals, trying to figure out why I had a Mexican family living with me on the ranch. None of it hurt me. I was used to gossip, with the most vicious of it coming from women my own age at the church. I quit letting it hurt me years ago. I'd become accustomed to the invitations not coming and the phone not ringing after I buried August.

Agent Cruz told me to stay quiet and at home with the family until he worked things out with the law on both sides of the border. He then put me in touch with immigration officials, so I could sponsor the Moraleses as lawful permanent residents, green card holders.

"It's a long process and expensive. We've got to prove the Morales family will be killed by the cartel if they return to Zaragoza. The fact their home was destroyed, Campos murdered by the gang members, are all evidence of that. It will take time. At one point, you'll go to court. There are lots of good immigration attorneys, Hannah, especially in Texas. Try not to worry."

I didn't worry. The one thing I learned from all of this was that worrying only made it worse. I stayed busy, pushing the what-ifs behind me. I never regretted picking up Ariela that night on the side of the road. It changed my life for the better. Seems like it all happened years ago. I knew it was against the law then, but I wasn't frightened of that. The only thing that scared me was not having the physical strength to do what needed to be done. That, and hurting Sam. But God help me, it was the first time I've felt alive since losing August. I'm not just existing anymore, sleep-walking through the hours until another day and night are done. I look forward to each new day, simply because my mind and body are still of use in this world. I have a purpose. I'd break the law again if it meant saving a life, not only Ariela's but mine, too.

Sam hasn't been to the house since I've been back, nearly two weeks to the day. He promised we'd meet today, in town at Vaquero's Café on north 377. Of course, that promise wasn't made over the phone. It was a text. His next text stated he'd never come to the ranch as long as the Moraleses were living here. Unwavering Sam. Made up his mind right away without talking to me, because he doesn't trust me. After all, I betrayed him and lied every step of the way in my dealings with the Morales family. I didn't have time or a choice; I had to rely on my instinct to survive and help them the best I could.

I only assumed the gossips in town were giving Sam information about the last two weeks. I don't think my brother Buddy would talk like that, but then again, I left Buddy holding the bag, too. Sam always trusted my brother. I'm sure he went to him for advice after he read my letter.

When Janie Pierce, a longtime friend, not necessarily a good friend, called me about it, I knew I'd better see Sam as quickly as I could so he could at least hear the truth.

Janie's version of my story was founded on the rumor I had Alzheimer's and hired the Moraleses to take care of me. It wasn't unusual for ranching families to hire illegals to work for them. That's been going on back and forth across the border for a hundred or more years.

But I decided to have a bit of fun with Janie, as I'm accustomed to dealing with people who think their intentions are good and consider themselves well-meaning friends. I satisfied her curiosity with a simple response. "Janie, how kind of you to be concerned. I must tell you I haven't been diagnosed yet, but I've been experiencing some memory loss lately. Like right now, as we're speaking, I'm having a hard time recalling how I know you."

My response took her breath away, as I heard a little gasp on her end. For a small moment, I actually regretted telling her that. After all, she was about my age with weight issues and high blood pressure, but my friend

Janie replied the way I expected her to, "Bless you, Hannah. I'll keep you in my prayers. Let me know if you need anything." And in less than a minute, she hung up the phone, so she could call another mutual, well-meaning friend with good intentions.

Janie and the others never mattered, but my son always did.

I have no problem leaving the Morales family here while I go to town. They are hard workers, good, decent people. It makes me happy to see Javier and Alicia playing with Ariela in the pasture near the house. Mr. Morales feeds the animals for me. I am thankful for the help.

Mrs. Morales stays near her family, and I hope she'll relax in time. It's hard to be in another woman's house, surrounded by her things, knowing everything you owned was a pile of ash in a place you'd never see again.

The Morales family were like every family in the world. They wanted to feed their children, earn a living, and have peace at home. It was something we took for granted in this country. Just like we quickly forgot those who died to give us that privileged life.

Uncle Rudy was a small-town boy who knew the freedom of open pastureland, the chance to work hard to get somewhere, the decision to live the life he thought was best for him. When he left the Divide as a young soldier to fight in Europe, he risked all he knew and loved for strangers, because he knew it was the only hope the human race had for survival. The stories of immigrants and soldiers were as old as time. It was still this country's story, whether people accepted it or not.

I was nearly in town when I thought I should call Agent Cruz with my plans. He wouldn't like it at all, but I'd only slip in for lunch with Sam and come on back, picking up a few things at the grocery store. I left the Moraleses with Sheriff Hoffman. He spent most of his time out on the ranch, now, protecting us. If he wasn't with us, he'd send someone in from the force. I couldn't imagine the hard time county officials gave him for wandering off to Mexico. But I never heard anything. Besides the call from Janie and three voicemails from my brother that I never returned, things were quiet. I'd go by and see Buddy, once I settled things with Sam. One relative at a time was always a good plan.

Maybe not many people knew the truth, the real story behind the Morales family and me. Little towns are like that out here in central and

West Texas. There's always going to be gossips, like Janie, but the people in the know, a few county officials, Sheriff Hoffman, respected families, they kept their mouths shut until you asked for help.

Most felt it wasn't anybody's business how we lived our lives on these ranches, as long as we treated people fairly and gave them a decent wage. People here cared little for Washington, DC, whose politicians cared little for us. The only time we heard from the federal government was when they wanted to recruit our young people for war or our taxes were due. Otherwise, we were too far west of the Beltway to matter.

––––––

Sam was sitting at a table near the hostess stand when I walked into Vaquero's. It was less than a month since I'd seen him, but he had aged like it'd been years since we last spoke. Dark circles under his eyes, the midsection paunch, all of it, gave the picture of a man defeated, something his father never felt or gave in to.

I spoiled Sam as a child. As an only child, he knew an easy life, one as a small-town prince, where everyone knew his mother and father, what they owned, and their influence in the community. It hadn't served Sam, the grown man, well. I also recognized I put him in the position of a failed man. I'm sure he thought I favored the Morales family over him, letting them stay out at the ranch with me. I hadn't forgotten how he wanted me to get rid of the ranch the day after his father was put the ground. I bet he hadn't forgotten it either.

His eyes met mine as I approached the table. They were sad eyes, crow's-feet fanning from the outer corners, puffy from too much drinking. His eyes said, "My mother lied to me."

"Don't get up, honey. I hope you weren't waiting too long."

I put my arm around his shoulder, then sat next to him facing the door, watching the coming and goings of small-town merchants getting a late lunch, the last of the Rocksprings Rotary members, leaving their monthly meeting held in the party room. A few I recognized, acknowledging them with a smile. In return I received the ranching man's sign of respect, a slight bow of the head with the index finger touching the brim of his cowboy hat, followed by my name spoken aloud, "Mrs. Durand."

"Mom, do you want to order first, or should we get the obvious out of the way? I don't want to upset you or ruin good Mexican food."

"Sam."

He looked down at the paper menu in front of him, then back at me, his eyes red.

"I'll never understand why you misled me. Never. It was the longest two days of my life, wondering where you were. If you were dead or alive. I couldn't tell Leslie and the boys. At that point, I just started lying to them. Leslie was on a wild goose chase trying to find you a retirement community in San Antonio. She also wanted me to talk you into selling the ranch. I let her do her research, so she wouldn't discover the truth. If she did find out, she'd want to know if it would be on the evening news, and how would she protect the boys from being embarrassed. Jesus, Mom. It's a mess. Now I learn you have these people living on the ranch. What the hell am I supposed to think?"

"I didn't raise you to speak to me that way. Now you settle down. Let's order some food and take this slowly. No one is talking about this in the press, and I don't think they ever will. You forgot how most decent people from here mind their own business. I understand you're hurt, but there should be no doubt in your mind I love you. You're my son. I carried you inside me for nine months. The Morales family is not going to replace that, Sam."

He quickly turned away, staring at the menu.

"Are y'all ready to order, ma'am?"

The waitress was a young girl, maybe sixteen, with one hand on her right hip and a smile revealing a row of braces. She was probably one of Juanita Cantu's granddaughters. Juanita and her family had been running Vaquero's for three generations.

"You want the chicken mole with the charro beans, Mom?"

"Been my favorite for a long time."

"We'll both have that. Bring me a Dos Equis in a bottle. Round of waters. Unsweetened iced tea for my mother."

It pleased me that he ordered for me, just like his father once did.

"Leslie and the boys okay?"

"Good at home and school. I know my face doesn't reflect that," he said, moving his hand through his hair. "I've just been worried, Mom. I don't know what your plans are with this family."

"I've been talking to a border patrol agent. We may be able to get the Morales family asylum based on the dangerous situation they're in. They're at the ranch because it's safe, Sam. I'd do it for anyone. I believe you'd do the same thing. That's the man you are. I hope that's what your father and I taught you."

"I understand, but, well, how realistic is this to take on at your age?"

"I'm not dead yet. I'm more alive than I've been since your father died. I have a purpose, and Sam, quite frankly, I can afford to do this."

The waitress delivered our drinks with chips and two small bowls of salsa verde and salsa rojo. Sam was intent on drinking his beer in one sip. I patiently waited, secretly hating that he felt the need to drink a beer like a man dying of thirst.

"What about the ranch?"

"Sam, tell me what you're really worried about. Do you think I'm going to give the Morales family the ranch? It's not going to happen. It's yours when I die, but I'm still very much alive. I'm going to enjoy my life out on that land, and the people who are in it, you, your family, the people of this town, and now, the Morales family. I'm not moving into an apartment off I-10 in San Antonio or to a retirement community, one step away from the cemetery. I want you to honor that, son."

"I just want to take care of you. Dad would want me to. I'm not trying to insult or control you, Mom. I'm trying to keep you out of harm's way, but you're bent on being right in the thick of things."

"I'll need you when that time comes. I take a lot of comfort knowing you'll be there for me." I reached across the table and squeezed his hand. He looked at me with tears in his eyes, his face red with embarrassment.

"Now, let me tell you about my crazy idea. I'm going to start a nonprofit for girls who have been taken from their families by bad men; girls who haven't had the same opportunities as you and me. The ranch will be a place they can visit for a couple of weeks, maybe longer, to heal. Enjoy the animals, nature. You know how special that land is. Why not share it with others?"

Our waitress returned with two hot plates of chicken mole, charro beans, rice, and corn tortillas.

"Well, you're not wasting any time, are you? It's your conviction on how you should live the rest of your life, no doubt."

"That's right, son. I need to do something with the years I have left, instead of waiting for you to come out with the boys and listening to the idle talk of old women at church. I wouldn't want you to live like that, and I know if you do a bit of soul-searching, you'll understand where I'm coming from. It's a good thing, Sam, to have a sense of purpose in life. Now, I've been studying the paperwork requirements with the IRS. I need your help in setting up the 501(c)3 for the nonprofit."

"Mom, I've got a choice here. Whether I help or not, I know it won't stop you. I'd rather be in your life."

"I promise not to wear you out. Don't want this getting in the way of your family life."

"You're my family, Mom."

We ate our meal with the comfort of small talk, the weather, the farm report, what my grandsons were doing. I knew he was still hurt about my decision, even confused, but all this would take time. That's something I had and would use wisely, as long as I could.

Before I left town, I picked up a few groceries for supper, a pack of dry black-eyed peas, gravy steaks, and onions. I had plenty of tomatoes in the garden for a fresh salad. Just as I was backing up from the parking lot at Lowe's, I saw Joseph's truck, next door at the feed and supply store. I drove there, parking next to him. I decided to wait until he came out. I hadn't seen him since we got back from Mexico, although he called, wanting to know if he still had a job out on the ranch. Everyone I knew thought they were being replaced by the Morales family. I told him to give me a few weeks to set a routine out there, but he still had a job on the ranch. Nothing had changed that.

Today would give me a chance to explain my plans for the nonprofit to him, without anybody interrupting or feeling left out. Joseph would be the best hire to build a bunkhouse for the girls. He'd help me buy a few more horses, build a new corral, so they could all have a chance to ride a horse while they stayed out here with me. I had the nicest thought of the girls naming the horses, like I did when I was a young girl.

I turned off the truck engine, rolled down the windows, watching customers come and go from the feed and supply store. Mostly men, buying feed, baling hay, even wire to mend fences; that's a job that never ended once you owned land, repairing fence line.

Joseph came out carrying a forty-pound bag of dog food, hoisted over his shoulder. I couldn't remember exactly how old he was, had to be pushing sixty at least, but he still carried his age well. Tall and slim, the body of a hard worker, no matter what age he was.

"Joseph, how are you?"

He looked in my direction, put the dog food in the back of his truck, and approached the opened window.

"Hannah."

"I've been working on some things. I'd like to hire you for a few building projects out on the ranch."

He walked over to the passenger door and got in the truck.

"I can help you with that, Hannah. Look, I've been wanting to talk to you about something since we got back from Mexico, but I didn't know how to put it out there. When we talked on the phone earlier, I didn't have the guts to say what needed to be said. But I'm glad to know I still have a job on the ranch. I guess this is the right time as any, but I think you know how I feel about you. Been feeling those things for a long time, since I was a kid."

I looked at him directly, and the intensity of his brown eyes met mine. I had no words for him. I couldn't even open my mouth to speak. My heart was beating so wildly, I could barely breathe in the cab of that truck with him in there with me.

"I know it will be a nightmare for Sam, maybe even my wife, but Elizabeth knows, has known a long time how I feel about you. I want to marry you. I want to live the rest of my days with you."

"Joseph."

He leaned into me, but I turned toward the open window on my side of the truck.

"I don't want to put you on the spot, Hannah. I know we're not kids. And I don't want to rush you with anything, but I have to tell you how I feel."

"I know," I said, not looking at him, because if I looked the confusion I felt would be written all over my face. I felt a sense of shame, thinking I had given this lonely man the impression I was interested in something more than our friendship. But I also was shocked, shocked at myself because I was thrilled that at seventy-three, a man could think of me in a romantic way. My god, what did it say about me and my forty-eight-year-old marriage to August, who been in the ground for less than a year?

"Don't make me feel like a fool for telling you, Hannah."

"You're not a fool. But it's not what you think it will be. It can't be. We'd lose a lot more than we'd gain in a few short years of being together. My son, grandsons, this town, people in it, though I really don't care what gossips say about me, but my family, Sam. They'd stop coming to see me. It would be too confusing for them. You'd lose your daughters, Joseph. They'd never forgive you for leaving their mother. I'm just not willing to make that hard bargain. You're a good man, Joseph. Any woman would love you the way you deserve to be loved. I'm just not that woman."

I turned toward him, shading my eyes with my right hand as the sun's glare reflected off the windshield.

"If you really think about it, I'm not such a good trade over a younger woman, Joseph. In a few years, my health will deteriorate. I'm a lot older than you, and that's just what happens when you get old: you start to die. I don't want to be a burden to you or anyone."

"You'd never be a burden. If bad luck found us, the good years would be worth the hard times. I'd take care of you."

"Joseph, what we did for Ariela, going to Mexico, helping the Morales family, has given me a new purpose. I want you to help me in my plans for the future, but I'll never marry again. You need to go home to Elizabeth."

He didn't say another word. The sound of the slamming truck door let me know the conversation was over and would never be brought up again.

CHAPTER THIRTY-FOUR

Hannah

Highway 377, near Junction, Texas

I guess I've failed the most important men in my life now by telling
them half-truths or not telling them anything at all, as far as my son
was concerned. But I never intentionally meant to mislead Joseph. My
conversation with him left me sad, but there was nothing else I could say to
him. He would have to mend his heart all on his own. To even attempt to
console him might be misunderstood by him, as well as Elizabeth. Opening a man's wound with a heart-to-heart talk with the woman who rejected
him would be humiliating, but I also knew the male ego and Joseph's
pride as a strong, working man. He might see it as a change of heart on my
part. There didn't need to be any more confusion between us, much less
the false hope of reading something more than intended by a look or a few
words from an old friend. I didn't want to hurt him. All I wanted was for
Joseph to go home to Elizabeth and maybe the two of them could work
on their marriage. He'd have to do the hard work with her, without me in
the middle.

Although Sam and I cleared the air at lunch, I knew there'd be resentment for a long time. I'd hurt him. It was as simple as that. I'd have to work
hard to regain his trust. The first thing I'd do was make him board president of the nonprofit. He'd know every transaction being made with the
money his father left me. As far as Leslie was concerned, I wished things
were better between us, but I had to accept the reality that had always been
there. She didn't like coming out here, and frankly, I didn't miss her when
Sam and the boys came alone.

I left my thoughts of Joseph and Sam as I drove out of town, making a
quick decision to not return to the ranch, because sadly, the most vulnerable

of the men I misled still hadn't heard from me. Travelling northeast on 377, it would take me less than an hour to be at Buddy's house, outside of Junction on the Edwards Plateau. It was still one of the prettiest places in the world to me.

I wasn't going to call Buddy and let him know I was coming. I knew he'd be home in the late afternoon. Our last conversation was a routine we set up, calling each other by eight in the morning, making sure we had made it through another night in our lives as widow and widower. Buddy had always been there for me, even when I was a kid, so it broke my heart knowing he was the last on the list to get an apology from me. I cringed thinking how he must have wondered why I didn't call him that very next morning at eight, after promising the night before I would. He left a voicemail on my cell phone, but I never listened to it. I couldn't bear to hear his voice full of worry and confusion.

It was a beautiful afternoon to drive with the sun centered high in a cloudless sky. August used to call days like this a bluebird day. It always made me smile when he said it.

I've made this route all my life and have never grown tired of it. The passing scenery was comforting, watching the gravel roads leading from 377 to a working ranch or small homestead. It was easy to differentiate the two. A ranch owned by a wealthy family had fine fencing, straight lines for miles and miles along 377. The cedar was cut and burned, replaced by green rolling hills and the grazing of cattle and exotics. Oak trees dotted those hills, section, after section, after section.

A poor family's ranch was chocked with cedar and mesquite. The fence line was an ongoing process. When you could afford to fix it, you did. Otherwise, you hoped everything would hold another year or two, because you were the one who pushed the post-hole digger, inch after inch, through the limestone-laced soil. When you couldn't dig anymore, you stopped, picked up a pickax and broke the rock before going farther with the digger. I saw my mother and father do that kind of work throughout their lives, their hands broken with arthritis and hard work. But they never complained. To own a piece of land to call their own was a gift they worked their entire lives to keep.

The land was green from a few unexpected spring rains. The rolling hills dotted with windmills, pumping water for grazing cattle and other livestock, was a daily reminder life here continued, despite the hardships of rock-filled dirt, extreme temperature ranges, and little annual rainfall. It was a life worth fighting for if it didn't break you, as it was for the people before my family, the Mexicans and American Indians who called it theirs long before the European immigrants and American sod busters.

Highway 377 was the connecting road between my life as the wife of August Durand and my life as the daughter of Arlene and Preston Schoen. My heart trembled when I realized they were all gone. Gone. Most of the time, it was too painful to accept the finality of death, no matter what age I was. My one consolation about being older and facing my own death was the years of familiarity I had with it. It wasn't a shock as I watched my body and mind move slower, with less energy and confidence in my physical ability. But there was never a time, no matter how many years I walked this earth, that I became accustomed to losing someone I loved. The loss was never filled.

I parked the truck underneath the crushed limestone driveway leading to Buddy's house. There was no dog to greet me. Buddy gave up his dogs years ago and took up with a cat one of his granddaughters gave him. I think Buddy and that old cat loved sharing the house together.

The closer I got to the front door, the more I saw the disrepair. The wooden front steps had visible holes from dry rot; the hand railings gave when I grabbed one for support; the entire place could use a fresh coat of paint.

The front door was open with the screen door latched closed behind it. The afternoon was already in the low eighties, so I couldn't imagine why he wasn't running the AC unless the bill was one more he couldn't handle on his social security check.

I stuck my face close to the closed screen of the door and called his name.

"Buddy. It's Hannah. Come on and let me in."

Rusty Bucket, the one-eyed yellow cat, made it to the door before my brother.

"Hannah, I'll be damned. You sure pulled a smart one on all of us. Where have you been, sister?"

"I've been to Mexico, Buddy. Now, if you don't mind putting the coffeepot on, I'll be happy to let you know the mess I got myself into."

I walked through the threshold of my brother's home and into his open arms. And I soaked up the love, unquestioning, unconditional, he gave to me, still the baby girl in our family mostly buried and gone.

"Now, I don't do much house cleaning these days, so don't start fussing with my stuff. Rusty and I like the way things are."

I removed a pile of newspapers, opened mail, and unfolded laundry on top of the kitchen table, placed them on the empty chair next to me, and sat down. Rusty was checking me out, running his crooked tail around my left calf, meowing with curiosity.

"He'll cover you with cat hair, Hannah. If you want him to stop, use that water bottle on the table and give him a little squirt. He'll leave you alone."

I laughed, watching my brother make a pot of coffee in the percolator I gave him nearly twenty years ago. It made me happy knowing it still worked. Stuff that works without trouble has always been a little miracle to me in everyday life.

"I'm going to give you the short version, Buddy. I don't know what rumors you've heard or who has called to ask about me."

"You don't have to explain anything to me. Yes, Sam did call me. Told me about the letter you wrote him. Then about everyone in Kerr and Edwards Counties was talking about the murder of the Mexican girl at the motel. I was afraid for you, Hannah. I'm not lying. Of course, I knew you'd come home, just like I know the sun is going to come up every morning. I've been waiting for you to call. So here you are, alive and in person. Now, that's a pretty darn good day in my book."

"I'm sorry I didn't call sooner. So much was out of control, and I had to think quick on my feet, which isn't so quick at seventy-three. Anyway, I have the Morales family out at the ranch now. I'm going to sponsor them for their green cards."

"August would have liked that, Hannah."

I began to cry, reaching for the cheap paper napkins my brother bought at the dollar store to spruce up his dining experience. Those things about Buddy, endearing, just like all those times he picked me up at the bus station when I came home from college. He was always happy to see me, no matter what mess his own life was in. I never once doubted his love for me.

He walked toward the table, placing a chipped saucer of dollar store cookies near the paper napkins, then slid a cup of black coffee in front of me.

"You know how news travels here, Hannah. That never seemed to stop you from living the life you wanted. It shouldn't stop you now."

"Wondering if you'd like to come out and stay with me at the house, Buddy."

"Sounds like it's full at the moment. Besides, my girls, grandkids might have a fit."

"Not now. I'll get Joseph to build a small place for the Morales family, once their paperwork goes through. I'm hiring the family to help me run the ranch, then I'm going to start a little nonprofit, something to help girls without much of a chance."

"Have you talked to Sam?"

"Right before I came over here. He'll help me, Buddy. I need your help, too."

"Don't know how this old man can help you."

"I need a friend, every day, in that house with me. Someone to have coffee with, share my meals with. The Moraleses are a family. They need their privacy and own lives. I want to respect that. Besides, I can't stand the thought of us living our lives hoping one of us will pick up the other end of the phone when it rings at eight in the morning, saying, 'Morning, looks like I'm alive for one more day.'"

"I don't want you taking care of me."

"Maybe I need you to take care of me."

"I understand what you're saying. We'd be better off with two, three years of drinking coffee at the kitchen table, together, than me trying to find a Western on TV and dozing off for the rest of the day in the recliner. My girls are always on me about that."

"Your girls are right, Buddy. What kind of life is that? You wouldn't have settled for that fifty years ago; why would you live without courage now, when you need it the most?"

"Well, I appreciate the offer, but I'm gonna have to think about it. Hard to move at my age. I know where everything is here."

"Keep your house. Let one of your grandkids live in it. Lord knows all these young families could use a break. Or keep it empty for when you get sick of me—you and Rusty can come back and enjoy the bachelor life, with no old woman telling you what to do."

"I kind of like that idea, Hannah. Now don't get your feelings hurt, but I've always kind of done my own thing. Just like you. It's how Mama and Daddy taught us to live."

I reached across the table to hold his hand in mine.

"I got some groceries out in the truck. Need to get them in your fridge. Probably should make a call back home, let Sheriff Hoffman know I'm here and will be back at the ranch before dark."

"Go ahead. Take care of your business. I'm going to find the dominoes. We'll get us a game going if you can stand being beat."

I walked through the screened front door, letting it close on its own, because I have always loved that sound. That and the rattling of dominoes on a wooden kitchen table.

CHAPTER THIRTY-FIVE

Hannah

Durand Ranch

Casa de Katia, a safe house for female victims of human trafficking, opened nearly three years to the day Katia Hernández was murdered. Our memorial day for her and the ribbon cutting for Casa de Katia was attended by Scott Hopkins, editor of the *Mohair Weekly*, my board of directors headed by Sam, Sheriff Hoffman, Agent Cruz, and Father Flores. Joseph and his wife, Elizabeth, as well as every member of the Morales family attended, along with Leslie and the grands. My Buddy, my sweet brother, wasn't part of today's celebration. He died a few months ago, during one of the coldest winters we've had in many years along the Divide.

Last February, on an icy morning, he walked to the mailbox for the weekly delivery of the *Junction Eagle* and slipped on the frozen porch steps. He reached for the post railing next to the stairs to balance himself, but that rotten post I had trouble with several years ago finally broke, causing him to fall off the porch, shattering his right hip and breaking his right arm. To this day I regret never fixing that railing for him, but what made it so bad for Buddy was he lay there for hours in the wet cold of that morning, waiting for someone to find him.

His oldest daughter Karla drove out to his place when he didn't pick up his cell phone after repeated calls from her. Karla found him unconscious in front of the house; his right arm was twisted behind his back. She still talks about Buddy's cat, Rusty Bucket, standing vigil at the front door. After the ambulance picked up Buddy, that poor cat went straight to Buddy's bed, refusing to eat or drink, until Karla asked if I wanted him. Of course I did.

Buddy didn't live long enough for surgery. In many ways, I think it was a blessing. Buddy would have been sent to a nursing home for at least a month of physical therapy. According to the medical team, he was too old and in too bad a shape to return to his own place and get home health care.

"If I can't be home, enjoying my peace and quiet with Rusty, what good is it to be bandaged up, sitting in a nursing home, waiting to die?"

He died in his sleep at the Junction Hospital a week later. The entire town of Junction went to his funeral. It was a testimony to the life he lived as an honest, hardworking man.

Although I never got to drink morning coffee with my brother, like we had promised each other, I did enjoy my coffee with Rusty purring in my lap. It was as close as I could get to having a visit and a cup of coffee with my brother.

I wanted to invite Katia's family to today's event, but Agent Cruz failed to locate them in Zaragoza. I'm sure they went into hiding a long time ago. They might be in Texas. No one really knew. I can only hope they escaped the suffering they knew in Zaragoza, moving far away to a better place, at least one where the children are safe and can attend school.

As I stood looking at the new buildings on the ranch and the faces of those who helped me create Casa de Katia, I was grateful, proud for all of us. Near the two bunkhouses Joseph built, establishing four separate bedrooms and two baths for the girls we hoped to comfort, I planted a rose garden for August, Buddy, and Katia. The Double Delight and Ballerina roses I chose for Katia thrived in that spot with eight hours of direct sunlight every day. In memory of Buddy, I planted yellow roses, bright Texas roses, with their color representing friendship, because he was one of my best friends from the time I was a just a girl, all those years ago in Junction on our parents' small ranch, to the day I shared my last cup of coffee with him. For the love of my life, August Durand, I planted crimson red roses, the lovers' rose, symbolizing my undying love to a good man.

Ariela helped me create a border around the rose bed with limestone rocks in different shapes. It was also her job to water them every day. Those roses in the hot Texas sun required one to two inches of water a day. In a climate as arid as ours, water was a luxury, and so were roses. Of all my trees, shrubs, and flowers planted on this ranch, the rose garden received the most care.

When all the work was finally done, paperwork, meetings, building projects shared by everyone standing near the rose garden today, I couldn't help but cry. I smiled through those tears, not brushing them away or hiding them, letting them fall down my lined faced to my neck. I was a strong old woman crying at the mystery of life, the tragedy and the beauty of it all.

In front of me stood the most beautiful example of that mystery, Ariela. She was wearing the white organza dress her mother made her for induction into the Rocksprings High School National Honor Society. Standing in front of the rose garden, wearing her new white sandals, her toenails painted purple, she was a vision next to the garden's colors of pink, yellow, and red blooms. The gold cross pendant around her brown, slender neck reflected the morning sun.

"Ms. Hannah, could you hold Perdita's leash for me? My little brother will let her roam all over the place while I'm talking. She just won't listen to him."

"Sure."

Perdita was a forty-pound, mixed-breed female the Moraleses adopted a few months ago. She was a lively gal for her size. It was only a few weeks ago we finally broke her of chasing the cows and horses out here. Although Perdita was a family pet, Ariela was the true owner. The two were inseparable. I'm sure Perdita reminded Ariela of Bolt and better times in Zaragoza.

Ariela handed me the leash, unfolded a sheet of white notebook paper she held in her closed hand, and began reading.

Dear Katia,

I know you are in heaven, looking at me, smiling, even joking at this dress I'm wearing. Telling me I am wearing a dress for a little girl, not a young woman. And then you would ask me why I was afraid of being a woman. You were always unafraid to say and do what you felt. It gave me a lot of courage.

Your strength was what I felt in me as I ran from the motel that night. It remained with me when I returned to Zaragoza, even when I started school in Texas. You were with me when I cried, struggling with English, afraid of being made fun of, always embarrassed when I sat in silence, confused by what others were saying. But I took my courage from you to finish the work, never giving up, because your chances were stolen from you.

Many people were looking at me, my brother, and sister for guidance, a path to be successful here, a different world, so unlike Zaragoza. I kept seeking your voice when I prayed every night for you. I was always hoping I'd hear you say you were proud of me, and I should keep pushing, ignoring the meanness of people who called me and my family wetbacks.

Sometimes I'd hear your voice in the wind out on the ranch, when I walked the pastures alone. Other times, your spirit would come to me when I saw a monarch butterfly kiss the petals on the wildflowers, knowing it had stopped just to see me, answering my prayer, as it continued its migration to Mexico.

When I get my high school diploma next year, I'll be sharing it with you. When I go to college, you'll be going with me. When I help girls just like us, I will think of you. You died, so I could live. Now, I live, so you will never be forgotten. I love you, Katia.

Forever, your best friend,
Ariela

She folded the sheet she read from into a square and closed her fingers tightly against it in her palm. When she stepped away from the center of the group, Father Flores led us in a prayer.

The last part of the ceremony was a ribbon-cutting in front of one of the bunkhouses with me at one end and Ariela holding the other end. Scott took a picture of us for the newspaper. I also asked him to take a picture of the Morales family in front of the rose garden, as a keepsake for me. They worked extremely hard to become citizens in this country. I was proud of them.

After the closing, Elizabeth approached me, stepping away from Joseph, who still didn't have much to say to me. The only consolation in the ending of our friendship was that he was living with his wife. I could live with him being polite yet distant from me. We would never be the candid friends we once were.

"Hannah, I want to thank you for the job out here. I'll love the girls like my own daughters."

"With your bilingual skills and knowledge of a working ranch, I couldn't think of anyone better for the job, Elizabeth."

I reached out to hug her and she returned the affection, but it was awkward for both of us. Maybe women never stopped competing, no matter how old we became, but I was relieved it was out in the open, and we were talking and working together. In time, she might relax around me, or our relationship would be like the one I had with my daughter-in-law—the strain would always be there.

"Are we going to wear some sort of uniform once things get going out here?"

"It's either blazing hot or a northern is raining hail on us, so layering clothes is best. I'm not requiring a uniform. The scorpions, rattlesnakes, poisonous spiders who live with us are just good reminders how important a pair of boots are. You know how it is out here. The only dress code we'll have is wearing ID tags the sheriff department will arrange, after we go through the FBI background check. It's my understanding that is done when an adult works with minors."

She turned her deep-set brown eyes at me, neither smiling nor acknowledging my ice breaker, but that was Elizabeth. And the reason I offered her the job. She wasn't a false flatterer with a hidden agenda. Elizabeth was plainspoken. She meant every word she said, or she wouldn't have said it.

"Joseph and I won't stay for cake, but I'll be out in a few days to stock the bunkhouse. Get the beds and bathrooms set up."

"Thank you. I don't know when Agent Cruz and the sheriff will connect us with the girls, but we'll be ready."

She walked away from me, her sleeveless top tight across her breasts, black jeans tucked into scuffed Ropers. She still wore her hair the way she did in high school, straight and jet black, with long strands of grey running through it. I always thought she was a stunning woman, even when she was just a teenager. The first time I met her was when she was pregnant with Joseph's child.

She was only a sophomore in high school. August and I were the only people to give them a combined wedding and baby shower. It was sad to me then, thinking how little they had to begin as husband and wife, plus as a father and mother. Joseph's mother, Benita Gonzales, came full of love and laughter. She couldn't have been happier for her son and welcomed her young daughter-in-law with open arms. She was a good woman in so many ways, always joyful despite being made a widow early in life and raising all her children on her own.

I don't remember Elizabeth's parents coming to the shower. In those days, it was a shameful thing to be pregnant out of wedlock. I never understood why people thought they were doing any good by distancing themselves from a young pregnant girl with hateful stares and critical words. As if that made anything better, especially for the young child coming into the world. People quickly forget their judgments, but the judged never forget.

Elizabeth was a proud woman then, and still was as I watched her walk side by side with Joseph to his truck, then drive away.

"How's it going for them?"

"Sheriff Hoffman. Good to see you on this day that finally came for us. Joseph and Elizabeth, well, I guess they're making it, just like the rest of us, one day at a time."

"He's a sensitive man, Hannah. Liz's a neglected woman. Perfect storm, but age makes us all a little wiser."

"I never figured you for a town gossip, Sheriff."

"Nature of my job."

He smiled as if he had something on me, but I didn't take offense. I knew he was a smart aleck, but he was also a friend, especially the last few years.

"Come on in the kitchen, Sheriff. Mrs. Morales made a tres leches this morning. I was lucky to get her. She opened a little bakery, Panadería por La Mañana, on North State Street. Best breakfast burritos. It's in an abandoned gas station Mr. Morales rehabbed. Did it all with the money he's made working with horses on the different ranches in the area. Same work he did in Zaragoza."

"I'm way ahead of you, Hannah. I get coffee and an egg and potato burrito every morning from Mrs. Morales."

"Good for you! I know there's quite a line in front of the front door on Sunday mornings, after nine o'clock Mass. Look, Sheriff, I've been meaning to ask you something about Agent Cruz. I've noticed he's very quiet around you, almost the exact opposite behavior when he visits out here with me."

"I have no excuses for Cruz. He's a lone wolf. Might be a personality disorder." He laughed when he said it, then headed for the house.

"Y'all join the sheriff in the kitchen for dessert and coffee before it's all gone. Please don't wait on me. I need to take care of something. It will only take a minute."

I watched them all walk past me; some I've known since I was a bride coming to this ranch. Others became part of my family in a few short years. Sam turned back at the porch and waved to me before walking in.

"Go on, son. I'm coming. Just a little slower than usual."

I thought of August, looking at that porch. The flood of memories gripping my heart like a vise as I pictured him sitting in the rocking chair, sipping a whiskey while I played my grandmother's accordion. His thought-ful gaze, his right hand on the whiskey tumbler, covered with brown spots, cuts, rough from all the years working the ranch in every kind of weather imaginable. I saw myself as a young woman barely out of her twenties, watching him watch me, loving me with his eyes, the middle-aged man who fathered our son. All too soon, he was an old man in that rocking chair, so brave throughout his life, even when it was slipping away from him.

The midmorning sun was burning off the haze of daybreak, warming the land as the heat rose through the caliche soil, filtering shadows under the oak tree I stood beneath.

August. Your name as familiar as my own, this air I breathe, the land we worked together. Sweetheart, I'm staying out on the ranch as long as I can. Doing good work with the money you left. Work you'd be proud of. I think it will heal Sam. Give him something besides a computer to stare at, might even bring Leslie around to loving this place. We could always hope for better. That's something you were very good at, hope.

I don't always know what life will bring me these days. Heartache, joy, Lord, even Mexico at seventy-three! But whatever it brings, I'll see it through. That's what we always did, August, lived our lives the best we could, loving each other every step of the way. I'm grateful for all those years together, loving you from the first kiss out at the river, to the last kiss the day we buried you. I've been a fortunate woman to know the love of a good man.

ACKNOWLEDGMENTS

I am indebted to the following authors and professionals for their time and wisdom spent on this novel: Jeannette Brown, Phillippe Diederich, Joanne Kukanza Easley, Pamela Lombana Livesay, Fernando Mejia, and Charlie Spillers.

ABOUT THE AUTHOR

A fourth-generation Texan, Johnnie Bernhard's family home is located 100 miles from the Texas-Mexico border. It is with reverence for the cultural diversity of this land she wrote *Hannah and Ariela*, her fourth novel.

Her first three novels, *A Good Girl* (2017), *How We Came to Be* (2018), and *Sisters of the Undertow* (2020), also explore the role of the immigrant in American culture. These novels have won the following literary awards and recognition: Robert W. Bingham PEN nomination; 2020 Press Women of Texas, first place; panels at state book festivals and the Pat Conroy Literary Center; shortlisted for the Wisdom-Faulkner prize; and chosen as the best 100 books published by a university press from the Association of University Presses, 2020.

Ms. Bernhard served as a TEDx speaker for the 2020 Fearless Women series. All of her novels are placed within the state library collection for the Texas Center for the Book.